DECEMBER

GABI SALAS

This novel is entirely a work of fiction. The names, characters and incidents portrayed in it are the work of the author's imagination. Any resemblance to actual persons, living or dead, events or localities is entirely coincidental.

Designations used by companies to distinguish their products are often claimed as trademarks. All brand names and product names used in this book and on its cover are trade names, service marks, trademarks and registered trademarks of their respective owners. The publishers and the book are not associated with any product or vendor mentioned in this book. None of the companies referenced within the book have endorsed the book.

Paperback ISBN: 979-8-9889056-3-9

If you read romance only to uncover new kinks, this one is for you. I hope you never look at the wind the same way again.

TROPES, TAGS, AND TRIGGER WARNINGS

Tropes:

Shape-shifting, chosen one, immortal love, paranormal, urban fantasy

Tags:

Guardians, magic, ceremonies, public sex, mind-to-mind communication, riddles, magical appendages, powerful women

Trigger Warnings:

This book uses explicit language and very descriptive sex scenes. Sex happens both privately and in spaces where other people are in attendance. The MMC is a shape-shifting wind who can turn himself into things for pleasure.

Oh my darling, cling to me
For we're creatures of the wind

NINA SIMONE

ONE

The unwavering woods whispered to young Itta Lyswyn. As a child, she would often wander among the trees, feet skimming the ground, following the sweep of the breeze and the pull of something far older than time.

Enchanted, she'd roam its hidden trails, her feet lightly kissing the ground, drawn by the tender caress of the wind and a primal allure older than history itself. When she traced her fingers over age-old bark, she sensed a rhythmic heartbeat, a thrumming life force that echoed her own lifeblood.

In the twilight hours, the essence of the woods danced around her. Leaves, invigorated by an unseen spirit, would pirouette in the air. Laughter, a soft and ethereal sound, seemed to emanate from the trees themselves, harmonizing with Itta's own mirth.

The woods had always protected young Itta Lyswyn.

There were times when, by the laws of nature, a misstep

should have resulted in pain. But whether she tripped over a gnarled root or leaped from a height, the forest cushioned her every fall. She traversed its expansive domain with a brave heart, every step taken with implicit trust. The woods embraced her like a parent cradles a child, soft and protective.

There was a moment when Itta got older that the woods came to her rescue in a fury. Unaware of the boys who had followed her through the worn trail and broken gate at the entrance to one of her favorite paths, Itta hadn't noticed them circling her until they'd cornered her in the dead end of a clearing.

She had stood in the center, her white dress blowing in the breeze as the boys had sneered at her and walked closer. Her eyes had darted through the trees hoping to spot someone, anyone to help her, but there had been no one.

Before the boys could even reach her, the ground shook. The Earth beneath their feet buckled and rolled, knocking the boys off their feet. Itta had stood in the center like a raised sentinel as the boys fell on their backs, rocks digging into their palms. The wind had come through the clearing in a howl, pushing back her hair in a swirl around her face.

The boys rolled toward each other in a clash and had to crawl over the Earth that still rolled beneath them. The Earth settled back in place after their footsteps faded through the woods. The wind died down back to a calm breeze, and the trees stood back upright after they had shaken violently in their places. It was as if the woods had breathed a sigh of relief at their exit. And so had Itta.

In the quaint farmhouse nestled at the woods' edge, Itta

often sought solace. Her mother, witnessing Itta's nocturnal sojourns, fondly dubbed her the "feral child." Many a time, in the embrace of twilight, she'd discover Itta asleep on a bed of soft moss, the moonlight casting ethereal shadows over her. With gentle care, she'd lift her daughter, bearing her back to their home. Yet, by dawn, Itta's bed was often empty, the call of the woods too potent to resist.

Serving as more than her refuge, the forest became Itta's confidant. Within its serene expanse, she'd recount tales of schoolyard adventures, the latest stories she'd read, and even the pesky bullies at the bus stop. In return, the woods would rustle its leaves in sympathy or send a gentle zephyr to console her.

As Itta got older, the woods called to her in new ways. There were evenings when she was trying to concentrate on a book or school paper, the silver light of the moon lighting the pages on her lap. Itta would feel an intense tingle, a kind of electricity that pulled at the core of her being. It would be impossible to ignore, and if she tried, the tingle would intensify.

Itta would set her schoolwork down and speak to the woods, "OK, fine, you've got my attention. What is it?" She could swear the woods smiled with her, happy she was finally ready to play.

A particular glade, where the moonlight was most concentrated, drew her time and again. With every step, the sensations heightened. The energy was seductive, warm, and inviting. It wrapped around her like the softest of veils, making her heart race.

Itta would stand in the center of the glade, stretching her hands toward the moon, her fingers dancing as if playing with the silvery rays. As she did so, the air around her shimmered and sparkled. She felt weightless, ethereal, as though she was both of the Earth and the stars.

She would stare in awe as her own skin seemed to sparkle in the moonlight. Her dress would blow in an invisible breeze, and Itta took it as a request. She would lift the hem of her dress, exposing her pale, bare skin to the night air. She could feel the deep sigh the woods would take whenever it would see her like this.

The more she surrendered to this newfound power, the more pleasure it brought her. She felt every sensation—the caress of the wind, the cool kiss of the dew, the soft murmur of the trees, and the distant serenades of the night creatures. Every touch, every sound, was amplified, filled with a sensuality and magic she had never known.

But with dawn's approach, the sensations waned. The tangible connection she had with the woods faded. Confusion clouded her mind. Was it a dream? A figment of her vivid imagination?

Itta would spend many nights after, seeking that very glade, chasing the magic that made her feel alive in a way nothing else could. She was destined for more, and the woods knew it. They had whispered their secrets to her, and she was ready to listen.

Once Itta's younger sister was old enough, she began taking her to the woods, to that glade. Itta needed to know if she was the only one who could feel it. Ondina would stand in the middle of the clearing, close her eyes, and stand very still. After a while she would shrug, looking at Itta curiously.

Getting tired of her antics, Ondina would run through the glade on bare feet to the trickling stream. Even when the water was ice-cold, she'd dip her toes in, swearing she couldn't feel the freezing temperature. Itta would walk along the water's edge as her sister would hop from rock to rock up and down the stream.

Where Itta's place was the Earth of the woods her sister's was the water of the stream. They both clung to their favorite places like a child normally clings to a blanket. Before long, their parents didn't even try to bring them back inside at night. Itta would watch over her sister as they both made their homes in the woods and along the stream, confident the woods would protect them both.

By the time Itta had graduated high school she could walk through the edge of the woods, past overturned logs, in between dense trees, and find the glade with her eyes closed. As if a thread went from her core to the center of that glade, it tugged on her, craving her.

So, night after night, she went. And every time the magic around her intensified. The magic didn't surprise Itta. Her mother came from a long line of women with curious traits. Magic helped run their farm and protected their land from unwanted visitors. Magic helped keep the house clean and created spreads of delicious meals for her family.

There had been rumors of women being chosen by the magic to live immortal lives. Her mother and aunt spoke of them for as long as she could remember. They were nonsensical choices. Sometimes their lineage would go decades without the immortal magic locking into place and sometimes there would be bursts of women blessed in a rapid pattern. Itta had pored over the records of these instances trying to make sense of it all.

Even though Itta suspected the woods must be a part of this magic, they were unable to answer her relentless questions about it. Itta would pace through the clearing, marking a path of worn-down grass with her feet, talking out loud.

"How does someone get chosen to be immortal?"

No answer.

"Can you submit yourself to be chosen?"

No answer.

"What is the purpose of being immortal?"

No answer.

But Itta could feel the magic flowing through her veins at that point. It was as if every time she visited the glade, she'd be replenished. Eventually, she was able to conjure magic by herself, showing off to Ondina and playing jokes on her parents. And so, to the glade she went. Day after day.

On the night of the Autumn Equinox, the year Itta turned eighteen, everything changed.

Aside from it being the longest night of the year, the evening was unlike any other. Itta had planned for an overnight in the glade. She'd packed a small rucksack of her things, a blanket, a book, and a few snacks. She'd walked, barefoot, her path lit by the light of the moon, and settled into the clearing.

After reading by moonlight, Itta had nodded off. And in

her sleep, she had dreamt of a creature. A creature the color of moonlight and the shape of a thick wind. A creature that didn't scare Itta, but instead, brought back a familiar tingle deep in her belly.

When the sunlight trickled in the next morning and the chirping birds woke Itta, her mind returned to the night before. When she had dreamt of a fog-like creature coming to her in her sleep.

In her dream, she could feel the creature watching her. As she slept, she sensed it weave in and out of the trees around the clearing before approaching her. She watched it bend and shape itself around Itta's sleeping body, slowly caressing her skin with a warm touch.

Itta sighed in her sleep at the pressure of the creature's touch. The foggy shape placed a heavy hand on her thigh. The tingling energy pulling Itta to the glade all this time was a tight thread between her and the creature. It zapped and fizzled like a current as the creature explored her.

Even though Itta had never met this unfamiliar creature, she had felt safe. The woods around her would've let nothing approach her without its approval. Itta remembered lying in the odd in-between of deep sleep and wakefulness. Every touch had felt *real* as the creature wrapped itself around her thighs and caressed her hips.

She lay peaceful now in the glade remembering the passionate tingle that had flown through her veins. Itta looked down at herself and her bunched up dress. She raised the hem of her dress and noticed the small red markings on the inside of her thighs where it looked like a hand had gripped her. And in between her thighs, Itta was still glistening from where she had found pleasure in the middle of her sleep with this unknown creature.

Besides the weird, but all-too-real dream, Itta felt different. Her skin glowed a bit brighter today, her cheeks felt a little warmer. As if something had locked in place last night, it gave Itta a new version of the world around her.

Itta gathered her things and headed back home.

Inside, the smell of a weekend breakfast filled the air. Bacon sizzled on a skillet and a heap of milk-soaked bread lay stacked on the table. Itta sat her bag down and slid onto the bench while she watched her mother in the kitchen. Itta had this feeling like she was watching everything unfold around her from some unknown perspective.

Her mother poured her a cup of tea and brought over the steaming mug, picking up an envelope off the counter.

"This came for you, dear," she said as she sat the mug down. "It looks like your cousin is—"

Itta looked up at her mother as she stopped midsentence, a look of wonder on her face. "What is it?" Itta asked.

"Your eyes, dear, you..." her mother smiled. "You've been made immortal."

TWO

"Hey, I got your mysterious invite, but it's oddly devoid of details. When exactly is your event?" Itta's voice wavered with a blend of excitement and confusion as she spoke to her cousin Sunday over the phone.

That morning, when her mother had caught the luminescent shimmer, the telltale sign of immortality, in the corners of her eyes, the air had grown thick with unspoken emotions. Breakfast felt surreal, every bite tinged with the weight of destiny.

The family's ancient record book, infused with its own kind of magic, updated automatically, reflecting each immortal's awakening. Itta anticipated an avalanche of phone calls, brimming with jubilation from family members spread across realms and ages.

Clutching the curious envelope, Itta ventured toward the woods, her phone delicately balanced in her other hand. She hoped the signal would persist long enough for her to pass the mystical tree line.

"What event?" Sunday's voice echoed with genuine surprise. Itta had a soft spot for Sunday. While others might misconstrue her quiet, somewhat aloof nature as standoffish, Itta found it endearingly authentic.

"Your invitation cryptically states 'Your Presence is Requested at Strange Mansion.'" Itta traced the ornate calligraphy on the front of the luxurious, cream-colored card stock. Turning it over, she continued, "And the back just reads, 'The Woods Are Calling.' Quite the riddle, wouldn't you say?"

A soft chuckle resonated from Sunday's end. "I genuinely have no idea, but I guess fate has its own designs. See you soon?"

Itta laughed, the sound as light as the flutter of wings. "Indeed. Perhaps your mom is behind this mystery?"

"No event I'm aware of, Itta," Sunday mused. "But our doors are always open for you."

"Thank you. I might just take up that offer," Itta replied, warmth flooding her voice. The Strange Mansion, sprawling and filled with countless hidden nooks, was a testament to their shared childhood. Memories of Itta guiding her younger cousin, Sunday, through its many forgotten rooms —each echoing with whispers of the past—filled her heart.

Lost in thought, Itta's mind drifted further down the corridors of time. She remembered summer evenings when the golden hue of sunset would filter through the stained-glass windows, casting kaleidoscopic patterns on the worn wooden floors. Together, she and Sunday would chase these dancing beams of light, their laughter echoing through the vast hallways.

Rainy afternoons saw them ensconced in the grand library, hidden between towering bookshelves, engrossed in tales of adventures and magic. They'd imagined themselves as the heroines of those stories, each room in the sprawling manse a backdrop for their fantastical journeys.

There were secret chambers they had discovered, the hidden nooks and crannies where they whispered secrets, shared dreams, and planned mischievous pranks. More than a building, the Strange Mansion was a living tapestry of their shared memories, each corner drenched in the essence of their intertwined childhoods.

And apparently it was calling her home.

With immortality on her side, Itta could always come back to these woods. *Her* woods. But standing here now, walking past the forest edge and deeper into its shadows, felt bittersweet.

She paused for a moment, allowing the woods to envelop her in its familiar embrace. As in the past, the sound of the wind whistling through the branches and the soft rustle of fallen leaves underfoot comforted Itta. Every step she took now was like a tribute, an intimate farewell to a dear friend.

On her left, the weeping willow near the pond waved its long tendrils, reminiscent of the countless times she had lounged beneath it, letting its drooping branches shield her from the world. The gentle ripple of the water, home to the fireflies she'd often chase on warm summer nights, reflected the willow's silhouette in a shimmering dance.

A few paces ahead stood the oak tree, its thick trunk bearing the engraved initials "I.L." This was where she had carved her name years ago, making her eternal mark on these woods. Itta placed her palm over the engraving, feeling the slightly jagged texture. This tree had been her silent confidant, absorbing her dreams and secrets within its bark.

As she ventured further, a familiar fragrance wafted in the air. The patch of wildflowers—violets, daisies, and lilies—painted a vibrant canvas on the forest floor. Each bloom held a story, from the violets she'd string into necklaces to the daisies she'd pluck for their petals, whimsically playing "He loves me; he loves me not."

And then, there was the clearing. The sacred space had been the center of so many mystical encounters. The heart of the woods. Rays of sunlight filtered through the canopy, casting a dappled pattern on the ground. Here she felt the most profound connection to the forest, its energy pulsating through her veins, grounding her and lifting her simultaneously.

Itta knelt in the center of the clearing, touching the soft Earth. Memories flooded back—of laughter and tears, of discovery and wonder. She whispered a soft "Thank you" to the woods, knowing this was not a final goodbye. It was merely a new chapter, a different path in the vast journey that awaited her.

Closing her eyes for a moment, the woods responded. The gentle breeze caressed her face, the birds sang a melodious tune, and the leaves rustled in acknowledgment. The woods would forever remain a part of her, and she, a part of them.

With a lingering glance, Itta rose and continued her walk, leaving behind the sanctuary that had shaped her. The woods had prepared her for this moment, guiding her toward the destiny that beckoned. And with every step, she moved forward with gratitude, anticipation, and a heart full of cherished memories.

The morning sun cast a cheery radiance into the Lyswyn household. The mellow chirps of the birds outside and the soft hum of morning routines provided a comfortable backdrop. There was an undercurrent of excitement, something new on the horizon.

Itta, glancing around the familiar setting, met Ondina's bright eyes. The younger sister's raven-black hair cascaded against her pale-blue dress. "So, off to solve the riddle at Sunday's?" Ondina asked with a teasing lilt in her voice.

Itta laughed, "Yes, it's intriguing, isn't it? 'The woods are calling.' Wonder what that means."

Ondina mockingly posed with a dramatic hand on her forehead. "It's a mystery most profound."

The two sisters giggled, their shared humor lighting up the room. After a moment, Itta grew a tad more serious. "Hey, while I'm gone, be careful around the stream. You know how it can get after the rains."

Ondina gave a playful salute. "Aye, Captain. Don't worry, the woods have got my back, remember?"

Their parents walked in, sharing amused smiles at the

sisters' antics. "Look at you two," their mother said, "always so protective of each other."

Itta hugged her parents. "It's just a visit, but it feels . . . important. Don't know why."

Her father patted her back. "Follow your instincts, Itta. They've always served you right."

With a final hug for her sister and a wave to her parents, Itta picked up her bag, her heart light with excitement. Whatever awaited at Sunday's, she was ready for it.

The journey to the Strange Mansion was a familiar one for Itta. As a child, the winding roads, the thick canopies shielding the sun, and the familiar landmarks signified an adventure. Now, driving in her compact SUV, she felt that same rush of excitement, underlaid with a new layer of contemplation.

She passed by Miller's Farm, where, as kids, they would stop to pet the calves and buy fresh milk. The old barn looked the same, painted red with white trims. Mr. Miller, albeit a bit older with more grays, still sat on his porch, waving to passing cars. She honked and waved back, his surprised recognition bringing a smile to her face.

Her mind wandered to the woods surrounding the Strange Mansion. Oddly, despite the numerous times she had visited, they had never ventured deep into those woods. Sure, there were picnics on the periphery, and games of hide and seek behind thick trees, but the deep heart of those woods remained unexplored. Now, with her newfound immortality, she felt a surge of curiosity about them. What mysteries did they hold? Were they similar to her own protective woods?

As the journey continued, she tuned into a local radio station, humming along to some old tunes. There was a lightness in her spirit, even as she pondered over her future. The car's dashboard blinked, indicating a need for fuel, and she pulled over at a quaint gas station.

"Headed to the Strange Mansion?" asked the elderly attendant, after noticing her direction.

"Yes," Itta replied with a chuckle. "I have family there."

The attendant smiled knowingly, filling up the tank. "It's an enigmatic place, that mansion. But then, the Strange family always did have an air of mystery about them."

Itta thanked him and continued on her way, the sun now beginning its descent, painting the horizon in a mix of orange and purples. The silhouette of the Strange Mansion appeared in the distance. The vast estate was even more magnificent than she remembered. The sun cast elongated shadows of the tall spires, and the ivy-covered walls looked even more mystical.

Driving through the ornate gate, she admired the meticulously maintained grounds. The fountain in the central courtyard was bubbling, its waters gleaming under the early evening light. The surrounding woods seemed denser, the trees older and more gnarled, creating an impenetrable wall around the elaborate dwelling.

Parking her SUV in the familiar circle drive, she took a

moment. With her immortality, every experience felt amplified. Itta eyed the tree line surrounding the property. The Strange Mansion was set high on a hill overlooking the desolate town below. A line of dense woods circled the back and sides. Itta could barely make out the trees past the first row in the early evening's dim light. She felt a small tug in her belly. The same feeling she experienced near her own woods back home.

For now, she got her bags out of the car, her cousin's family's butler coming out to help her. Her aunt Tish stood at the door in a long black silk dress, her pale skin creamy against the fabric and her red nails sharp.

"Hello, dear, welcome back. We missed you," her aunt spoke into her neck as she hugged her tightly.

"Thank you for having me," Itta replied.

With one last glance over her shoulder at the woods, Itta stepped inside.

Where Itta and Sunday's maternal line was magical and immortal, Sunday's paternal line was . . . eccentric. Sunday's father traveled the globe and collected oddities he found tucked away in spaces most people wouldn't dare step inside.

At this point, Itta wasn't fazed by the specimens in jars or the glowing liquids that swirled in containers. The framed skulls or eerie sketches hanging from the walls didn't creep her out. Even the odd collectable that scurried around the dining table and seemed to care for Sunday didn't bother her.

Itta simply sat at the dining table surrounded by her family and smiled. The world they were a part of wasn't like anyone else's and that made it even more special. She didn't know why the invitation was calling her to the Strange Mansion, but she was more than ready to dive in and find out.

Itta wondered whether, here in a new place, she would dream of the foggy creature again tonight.

Morning light seeped through the curtains of Itta's room at the Strange Mansion. She felt a peculiar tug, like the gentle insistence of a magnet. The woods beckoned her again. But this wasn't the familiar call she was accustomed to from her own woods. This one felt more cryptic, deeper, and more mysterious.

Itta dressed in wool leggings and an old sweatshirt before tugging on fleece-lined boots. Autumn was starting to close, and the winter season would soon bring in a frost. She could see the chill in the air creep in through the frost lining the edge of the windows in her room.

Itta had taken up her old room on the second floor of the Strange Mansion. She looked around the room she hadn't occupied in almost a year. Trinkets from her and Sunday's adventures around the property littered the dresser's edge. Rocks and pebbles stolen from the creek's edge, feathers snatched off the path, and old flowers lay pressed between pages.

The room was an odd reflection of her childhood whims and her newfound freedom of, not only an adult, but an immortal one. Itta knew Sunday wouldn't rise for a while.

She was a night owl through and through, and even on her best day, would never be described as a morning person.

Itta filled a thermos of tea from the kitchen, grabbed a piece of buttered toast, and headed out through the back terrace to visit the woods.

The woods behind the Strange Mansion were vastly different from those back home. The trees here stood taller, their boughs forming intricate canopies the morning sun dappled through. The sunlight created an intricate dance of shadows and beams on the ground beneath. The closer Itta got, the more the air changed, becoming denser with the Earthy aroma of moss, dampness, and age-old bark.

Every step on the woodland floor felt like a soft caress. The ground was carpeted with fallen leaves in a myriad of colors, from amber and russet to deep shades of burgundy. They crunched softly beneath her boots, their scent adding to the rich jumble of woodland fragrances. Occasionally, she'd step on a patch where mushrooms sprouted, and she'd feel the sponginess underfoot.

The sound of distant woodland creatures playing their morning tunes filled her ears. Birds chirped harmoniously, their songs creating an orchestra with the occasional rustling of a squirrel or rabbit dashing through the underbrush. The woods were alive, and every creature, from the tiniest insect to the majestic stag, had a part to play in its symphony.

With every step, memories of her childhood visits here with Sunday resurfaced. They'd played hide and seek, built forts, and, as they got older, shared secrets. But they rarely ventured deep into these woods. They respected the invisible boundary, like a line etched in their minds they dared not cross. Now, she felt an inexplicable urge to go beyond, to delve deeper and uncover the secrets the woods held.

As she wandered, that peculiar pull intensified. It wasn't forceful, but it gently guided her. Trusting her instincts and the tingle in her veins, she let herself be led. Every so often, she'd stop, close her eyes, and try to sense the direction in which the magnetic tug was strongest.

The deeper she went, the more she realized how little she had truly explored these woods during her childhood visits. Twisted trees with gnarled branches reached out, as though whispering ancient secrets. Some of their trunks had old carvings, likely etched by generations before her. There were symbols she recognized from the stories her mother told—sigils of protection, love, and guidance.

The woods changed the deeper she ventured. Sunlight found it harder to break through the dense canopy above, casting dappled patterns on the woodland floor below. Ferns and moss carpeted the ground, and occasionally she'd come across a brook with water so clear it looked like flowing glass. The gentle babble of these streams provided a calming backdrop to her journey.

At intervals, she'd find peculiar landmarks—a circle of mushrooms, a particularly twisted and knotted tree, or a patch of flowers that glistened. Were these mere quirks of nature or markers set out for her? The idea the woods might be aiding her quest gave her a strange comfort.

The pull led her to various parts of the forest, but never to a defined endpoint. Like a game of hot and cold, she sometimes felt she was on the brink of discovery, only for the sensation to diminish, guiding her in a different direction.

The forest was a labyrinth, and she was both lost and found within it. The sweet scent of pine and cedar filled her senses, and the occasional rustle of an unseen creature reminded her she wasn't alone. The woods were watching, waiting, and guiding her dance within them.

As the sun rose high in the sky, barely trickling down through the tops of the trees, Itta made her way back. The play of shadows and dappled sunlight on the woodland floor created a mesmerizing, hypnotic pattern she found herself getting lost in. The muted chirping of birds and the distant whispering of leaves formed a serene soundtrack to her reflections.

There was an undeniable sense these woods held a secret for her alone. A place or a moment she was destined to uncover. The gentle pull she had felt earlier seemed like a nudge from the universe, guiding her toward some hidden truth. Yet, every time she thought she was close to discovering it, the sensation would change, leading her in another direction.

With every step, she pondered the bond she felt with these woods, different from the one she shared with the forest near her family's home. This was a connection forged by destiny, not just history. It was as if these trees, this Earth beneath her feet, had been waiting for her, guarding a secret only she was meant to unEarth.

The urgency of this mission, though unclear in its specifics, weighed on her heart. Why had she been chosen?

What did the woods see in her that made her the torchbearer of this quest? She had always felt a kinship with nature, but this was deeper, almost primal. A call she couldn't ignore, this was a responsibility she didn't fully understand but felt compelled to honor.

Despite the seemingly endless expanse of time that immortality offered, Itta couldn't shake the feeling of urgency. The woods, in their timeless wisdom, signaled that something pivotal was on the horizon. Something that required her attention sooner rather than later.

As she neared the edge of the woods, the imposing facade of the Strange Mansion came into view. The grandeur of the mansion, with its intricate designs and storied history, felt both imposing and comforting. It stood as a testament to her family's legacy, and she felt a renewed determination to solve the enigma the woods presented.

Upon entering the mansion, the warmth of the indoors and the familiar smell of age-old wood enveloped her. It was a sharp contrast to the crisp air and Earthy scents of the forest, yet it felt like home.

Sunday, hearing her entrance, came down the grand staircase, her curiosity evident. "Did you find what you were looking for?" she inquired.

Itta sighed, "Not yet. But I feel like I'm on the cusp of something significant. There's a mystery in those woods, waiting to be unraveled."

Sunday's eyes gleamed with understanding. "The woods have their ways, their own timeline. But if they've chosen you, then there must be a reason. Trust in that."

Itta nodded, taking solace in her cousin's words. She might not have all the answers now, but she was on a path, and she trusted that, in time, the woods would reveal their secrets to her.

***

The darkness of the night wrapped around the Strange Mansion like a cloak. The ticking of an ancient grandfather clock echoed down the hallways, marking the passage of time. Itta had retired to her room, the weight of the day's reflections making her eyelids heavy. The softness of the bed and the comforting scent of aged wood and floral perfume quickly lulled her into a deep sleep.

In the world of dreams, a surreal mist enveloped her. The once-familiar surroundings of her room melted away, replaced by a dense forest bathed in silvery moonlight. The air was thick with anticipation. The forest came alive, its every rustle, chirp, and whisper forming a symphony of expectation.

From the depths of the mist emerged a form, elusive and constantly shifting. Its presence felt familiar. The boundaries blurred between it and the mist, making it difficult to discern where it began, and the night sky ended. Its ethereal form swirled and danced, taking on humanesque shapes and then dissipating into wisps.

This was the creature that had visited her in her dreams not long ago. On the night she was made immortal. The same feeling of safety wrapped around her. This creature wouldn't hurt her. In fact, she subconsciously relaxed as its form flowed around her, caressing her exposed skin.

Itta sighed and rolled onto her back as the creature's form grazed her thighs. Even though she *knew* she was still in her bed, she could feel the soft push of the dirt on her back as the creature added pressure to her hips and waist as it roamed over her.

This creature was barely touching her, but Itta felt a tingle of energy throughout her body. Her blood vibrated; her breath felt heavy. When the creature hovered over her, she finally braved a look.

Eyes, a deep shade of indigo, materialized from the mist, locking onto Itta's. Those eyes held the wisdom of ages, mysteries of the cosmos, and a seductive allure impossible to resist. They bore into her soul, making her heart race.

Itta felt a surge of emotions: fear, intrigue, and an intense yearning. The foggy form drew closer, its cool touch sending shivers down her spine. As it circled her, its presence was both intimidating and intoxicating. The forest held its breath, amplifying the electric tension between them.

Suddenly, it was right before her, its misty form inches from her face. Its voice, a blend of a whisper and a hiss, caressed her ears. "Awaken, Itta."

The words reverberated within her, shaking her core. A sense of urgency in his voice conveyed a plea wrapped in a command.

Startled, Itta sat up in bed, her heart pounding in her chest, the sheets falling from her naked body. The room was steeped in shadows, the curtains gently swaying with the breeze. The dream, or vision, had felt so real, so tangible. The lingering sensations on her skin and the echo of the creature's deep voice in her ears made her question reality.

Trying to shake off the lingering feelings, her gaze fell on her travel bag, discarded at the foot of the bed. Compelled by an inexplicable urge, she reached inside and pulled out the mysterious invitation she had received.

The elegant calligraphy that had previously adorned the card seemed to have shifted. The previous message was replaced with a cryptic phrase: "Seek the root to find the truth."

The weight of the dream, combined with the changing invitation, sent a rush of adrenaline through her. There was no denying it now. The woods, the mansion, and even the depths of her own dreams were guiding her toward something. And the creature, the enigmatic entity from her vision, was a key piece in this puzzle.

Itta leaned back against her bed's headboard, trying to calm her racing mind. The blend of fear, excitement, and anticipation swirled within her. As the first rays of dawn swept through the curtains, she realized her journey into the mysteries of the Strange Mansion and its surrounding woods had only just begun. She was destined for a quest, one that would challenge her understanding of her family, her legacy, and her own place within it.

To Aether, the Ancient Watcher,

The pull grows stronger with each passing moon. She's here, teetering on the edge of destiny. With her arrival, hope blossoms. Yet, she remains unaware of the gravity of our bond.

The Eirelyn legacy and the balance of our realms rest on her shoulders. The woods resonate with anticipation. Guide her steps, Aether, for without her, our world risks fading into obscurity.

Till our realms converge,
S.

FOUR

Itta awoke, the pre-dawn darkness enveloping her room. It wasn't the sun that roused her, but a soft, unyielding pull—a tug at the core of her being that beckoned her to the woods. The memory of the newly revealed clue from her invitation flashed in her mind. Driven by a desire to unravel its mysteries, she rose.

In the quiet of the early morning, with the household still immersed in slumber, she moved around, gathering essentials. She filled a thermos with the fragrant herbal tea that kept her warm during her forest excursions. Packing some bread, cheese, and dried fruit, she prepared for a day's journey. Pulling on a thick woolen sweater and wrapping a scarf snugly around her neck, she braced herself for the winter chill.

Exiting the mansion, she hesitated. Instead of being led to the familiar entrance of the woods she knew so well, the pull directed her toward a lesser-trod path. Itta's curiosity piqued. Trusting the guiding sensation, she ventured forward.

The landscape of this new path was unlike anything she'd ever seen. The ground, covered in a thick layer of brown and golden leaves, rose and fell in undulating hills. Tall pine trees stood as silent sentinels, their tops lost in the low-hanging morning mist. The air, thick with the scent of damp Earth and pine, was punctuated with the distant sounds of forest creatures starting their day. It was as if she had stepped into an entirely different realm.

As she trekked on, the sky changed. Purples and deep blues made way for oranges and pinks. The sun began its ascent, and contrary to Itta's expectations, it wasn't the crisp winter morning she had dressed for. The day quickly warmed, the sunrays filtering through the trees, casting intricate patterns on the forest floor. Removing her scarf and unbuttoning her sweater, Itta marveled at the unexpected warmth.

By mid-morning, she felt the need to rest. Finding a smooth boulder, dappled in sunlight, she settled down, unpacking her food. The cheese and bread, paired with the sweet, dried fruits, nourished her body, but her mind remained restless, hungry for the answers that eluded her.

She let her gaze settle over the woods around her, taking in this new area with interest. Itta was restless to unravel the clue. *"Seek the root to find the truth."* What does it mean? What root does she need to find? This forest had to be full of millions of them.

Lying back on the boulder, she let the sun warm her face.

Itta slid off her sweater and bunched it up beneath her head. Her neck and belly lay exposed to the sunlight with her small periwinkle bralette covering her chest. Her eyelids grew heavy, and she drifted, not into sleep, but into that curious space between wakefulness and dreams.

And there he was, the ethereal fog-like creature, swirling around her. Itta was at least able to call it *him* now that he had spoken to her last night. The memory of his deep voice vibrating through her core stirred something in her. In this dreamscape, the woods around them grew dense and dark, the sun obscured.

The creature's presence was at once haunting and comforting. Closer now, his misty form circled her, brushing against her skin, leaving a trail of tingling sensation. The misty fog of his body took shape at his command. The near-sheer color of him felt solid against her neck as he grazed her.

Itta tilted her chin up to the sky, craving more of his touch. He obeyed. He formed a section of his body into a hand and trailed his fingers down her throat and between her breasts. Goosebumps prickled her skin, and his fingers slid down to her belly button.

Itta couldn't decide if this was real or part of her dream. Maybe she hadn't gotten much sleep after his visit last night and was now in a weird state of consciousness. But he felt *real*. Especially as his fingertip trailed between her skin and the band of her pants. She reached down and slid the stretchy material over her hips.

She lay on the rock now, exposed for this creature in the heart of the forest she'd never seen before. Itta could *feel* his approval as if he spoke it to her in her mind. She smiled and widened her legs for him.

"Are you real?" Itta whispered, her voice echoing in the strange dream.

The creature paused. "Tell me if this feels real." Itta heard his voice rumble in her mind, and she released a gasp as she felt two thick fingers slide down her middle.

"Yes, I feel that." Itta nodded and let out a deep breath.

"And what about this?" the creature asked as it slid those fingers past her folds and into her warmth. "Does this feel real?"

"Oh my god, yes." Itta was breathless as the creature used its large fingers to pump in and out of her.

"Oh, Itta," the creature said, "you feel like home."

The creature was stretching her, filling her deeply with impossibly long fingers. The rest of its wispy form floated around him, and Itta wondered what other forms he could take on.

She heard the creature chuckle in her mind. "One day, Itta, you will see. For now, come for me."

Itta wasn't sure how he could hear her thoughts or how she could hear his. But his fingers continued their ravaging. Itta was dripping wet. She could feel herself. Hear herself. And as the tension in her belly built, the creature's fingers thickened even further.

She grasped onto his hand and held it still as she ground herself into his palm. Itta's legs tightened and shook as the orgasm racked through her body. Once she came down from the high, he grew smaller inside her so he could pull out his fingers. She felt his hum of approval deep in her mind.

"Who are you?" Itta thought.

But instead of a direct answer, she felt a rush of emotions —yearning, anticipation, and an urgency she couldn't quite place. The woods, the creature, and the clues—they were all connected, pieces of a puzzle she was destined to solve.

As quickly as the dream came, it faded. Itta's eyes fluttered open to the sunlit woods around her. The vision of the creature remained imprinted in her mind, a specter guiding her journey. She sat up and tugged her leggings back up, smiling at the glisten that stained the inside of her thighs. Itta shook out her sweater and tied it around her waist before gathering up the rest of her things.

The first clue was still an enigma, but she felt closer to the answers. Following the persistent pull, she continued her quest into the heart of the woods.

As Itta's feet crunched on the bed of dried leaves and twigs, her thoughts raced. Each step she took resonated with a rhythm, an ancient heartbeat of the forest. The pull grew stronger, more insistent, leading her deeper into the woods.

Before long she reached a dense part of the forest where the trees seemed older, their trunks gnarled and twisted, their roots surfacing like serpents from the Earth. Sunlight filtered in patches, casting an ethereal glow around. A peculiar root caught her eye, distinct from the others around it. It rose from the ground, twisting upward and curving in a way that made it look almost like a question mark.

Itta was drawn to it. As she approached, she felt a vibration, a gentle hum emanating from the root. Tentatively, she reached out, and the moment her fingers brushed its surface, a flood of images and emotions washed over her.

As she touched the root, fragmented visions danced before her eyes. Silhouettes of people moved gracefully through the woods. Their purposes and intentions remained shrouded in mystery. There were fleeting images of past family members, some recognizable from old photographs and stories, all of them seemingly drawn to or engaging with the woods in some significant manner. Flashes of a magnificent clearing bathed in moonlight peppered her visions, but its significance eluded her.

Whispers of laughter, chants, and conversations flowed around her, but she couldn't grasp their full meanings. Each vision was like a puzzle piece, distinct and unique, yet she couldn't quite see the full picture they were meant to form. They all breezed through her mind in rapid succession.

A feeling of profound connection washed over her, but with it came a barrage of questions. Why was she seeing these images? What did they mean? Why her? The visions were intriguing, filled with beauty and mystery, but they left her with a thirst for understanding and a desire to delve deeper into the tapestry of her family's history and its bond with these enigmatic woods.

Tears streamed down Itta's face, not of sadness, but of belonging. The root wasn't just a clue. It was a conduit, a bridge to the collective memories of her lineage and the magic they shared with these woods.

She sat there for what felt like hours, absorbing, learning, and understanding. The urgency she felt earlier now had meaning. The woods weren't just calling her; they were entrusting her. She was chosen not merely because of her lineage but because of her innate connection and understanding of nature's rhythm.

Amidst the flurry of visions and emotions, Itta pieced together something deeper, something foundational. Was it possible these woods were the source of her family's magic? Taking their powers for granted, she'd never questioned their origin. But the secrets hidden within the woods and the beckoning pull she felt toward them now seemed to be revealing some truth. Was the magic in danger? Did the woods need protection, and was that her role now?

These questions danced in her mind, intertwining with the memories and images she'd witnessed. The realization she might be a guardian, as those before her, dawned on her. A protector of an ancient magic, a preserver of a legacy that ran deep in her blood.

More significant than being immortal or having magical abilities, it was about understanding where those powers came from and ensuring they continued to thrive for generations to come. The weight of this responsibility pressed on her, but it was a weight she willingly accepted.

The woods had whispered secrets of the past to her, and now they entrusted her with their future. This thought overwhelmed and humbled Itta simultaneously. Her destiny was intricately woven with that of these woods.

Gathering herself, she rose from her spot, giving a nod of gratitude to the root, which had initiated this journey of revelation. She felt a profound connection, not just with the present woods, but with its entire history, and with all those who had walked its grounds before her.

She didn't have all the answers yet, but she was determined to uncover them, to understand her role fully, and to ensure the magic and mystery of these woods remained undiminished. The path ahead was uncertain, but with the woods by her side, Itta felt ready to face whatever lay ahead.

Itta didn't know what role the creature played, or what his name even was. Do creatures even have names? Would he be offended if he knew she was referring to him as "creature"? Nor did she know why she had been chosen to fulfill this mission. Something in her bones told her, whatever it was, had great impact.

But what she did know, deep down, was that the creature would be her guide on this journey. He was a connection to whatever she needed to figure out.

To Aether,

Each day that passes, the weight of millennia rests heavier upon me. The eons I've spent in solitude, guarding, waiting, and longing for the one who would once again resonate with the ancient song of the woods. Today, Aether, I felt it—the undeniable bond that entwines our fates.

She came to me, raw and open, her spirit resonating with the very core of the woods. And in her presence, my restraint wavered. I touched her soul, mingling our energies in a dance as old as time. The intimacy was unlike anything I've ever experienced, the mingling of ethereal and mortal, of guardian and chosen.

But with this connection, a pang of guilt and fear now gnaws at me. Have I over-stepped? My many forms, shaped by the magic of the woods and the duty I bear, are not always gentle or comprehensible to mortals. I hope, deeply, that she isn't afraid of what I am, of what we might become together.

If only she knew how this bond, while

surprising for her, has been a yearning that's haunted me for eons. I've waited for her, for this moment, ever since the last guardian's song faded into whispers. She is here now, and I can barely contain the surge of hope and anticipation.

But as always, there is a purpose, a higher calling, and a duty that transcends even the deepest desires. I hope, in her heart, she understands what we share is more than intimacy—it's a union of destinies. A merging of old and new, past and future.

Soon, she will fully grasp the importance of her role and the sacred duty we share. Until then, I can only hope she feels the sincerity of my intentions and the depth of the connection that is blossoming between us.

Always in wait and hope,
S.

SIX

Late afternoon sunlight bathed the Strange Mansion in a warm, golden hue. Itta, still weary from yesterday's exploration and the tumult of emotions it unEarthed, slowly descended the staircase. Her night had been restless, with dream fragments flashing like a broken kaleidoscope—whispers from the woods, riddles without answers, and the longing for that elusive, misty guardian.

Yet, as dawn approached, a calm heaviness enveloped her, lulling her into a deep sleep. As if a gigantic, weighted blanket had laid over her, it calmed her nerves and limbs. She had hoped, even prayed, it was the creature's touch. *If only I knew his name.*

She walked past Sunday's room, peering through the slightly ajar door. Sunday was engrossed, buried behind mountains of files and folders, her raven hair cascading around her face like a protective shield. Itta could sense the concentration radiating from her cousin, so she decided against disturbing her.

Making her way to the kitchen, she prepared a plate of sandwiches and a cup of tea. The idea of diving deep into her maternal family's history and understanding more about her lineage had been tugging at her all day. They never discussed it openly, and like many things in the Eirelyn family, the magic had always just been . . . there. Accepted but not truly comprehended.

And maybe because it had been taken for granted for eons was why she felt this pull now. Had anyone ever considered where it originated from? Or an even bigger question . . . how was it maintained?

With her food in hand, she directed her steps toward the library. The mansion's library was an architectural marvel. Situated on the main floor, its tall, oak double doors stood guard like silent sentinels. As she pushed them open, the scent of old books—leather, paper, and a touch of mustiness —filled her nostrils. Towering bookshelves lined the walls, their wood darkened by age and polished to a soft shine. Ladders on wheels were placed strategically, allowing access to the higher shelves, and plush armchairs beckoned, nestled in corners with reading lamps poised overhead.

Itta recalled rumors of a second library somewhere on the third floor, but that space had been off-limits for as long as she could remember. Whispered legends painted it as a repository of arcane knowledge and forbidden rituals. But today, her quest was in this library.

She slowly walked between the shelves, fingers trailing

along the spines of ancient volumes, her mind a whirlwind of thoughts. Somewhere here lay the answers she sought, clues to the magic that ran in her blood and the mysterious guardian of the woods.

Selecting a few promising titles, she settled into one of the armchairs, letting the library's comforting atmosphere wash over her. The soft creak of leather, the rustling of pages, the muffled ticking of a grandfather clock—these were the sounds of a sanctuary, of a room that had seen countless hours of study and introspection.

She delved into a book detailing the origins of the Eirelyn family, hoping to find a hint, a reference, anything that might shed light on the woods' guardian and the bond he shared with her lineage.

But, as with any quest, it wasn't going to be easy. The library, however, seemed ready to guide her, each book a stepping stone on her path to discovery.

The sun was now a faint ember in the sky, and the library's vastness enveloped Itta in a blanket of shadows and soft luminescence from the few candles she had lit. Her fingers skimmed over the time-worn spines of ancient tomes, their stories filled with magic, mysteries, and histories she had never before realized were so vast and complex.

Feeling that tug deep within her, Itta closed her eyes for a moment, letting the sensation guide her. There was a playful essence to it, making her think of hide-and-seek, a game of hot and cold. The pull grew more potent as she neared the tall mahogany ladder. Climbing a few rungs, her fingers settled on a particular volume askew from the others.

Deciding to voice her feelings, she whispered, "If this is your doing . . . thank you." She felt a little silly speaking to seemingly no one, but right away, the air around her grew warmer. The once-dwindling fireplace roared back to life, the flames dancing with what appeared like joy. Chuckling to herself, she remarked, "Talkative, aren't you?"

She took the book in her hands and descended the ladder. The title, etched in gold against the worn leather, read: *Guardians of Aeon: The Eternal Balance.*

Opening the tome, she delved into the lore of the guardians. These mighty entities, each tied to a fundamental element, held dominion over vast regions. There were the keepers of Earth, steadfast and enduring; the sentinels of Water, deep and ever flowing; the protectors of Fire, passionate and volatile; and the guardians of Wind, elusive and free.

Her creature, she realized, was of the Wind. His essence was that of the breeze, the gust, the gentle zephyr, and the raging tempest.

But as she continued to read, she discovered that for all their might and dominion, each guardian bore a vulnerability. The balance of power was perpetually at risk, with guardians constantly under threat of being overwhelmed by neighboring entities from the same element seeking to expand their territories and influence.

The text delved deeper, speaking of rites and rituals the guardians could undertake to fortify themselves against such incursions. Most significantly, there was the ancient rite of bonding—a merging of essence with a chosen mate.

This bond amplified their innate powers and solidified their post, ensuring their dominion remained unchallenged.

Itta traced the words with her fingers, a realization dawning. She thought of the guardian in the woods, the intimate encounters, the deep yearning she felt. "Is this our destiny? Are we bound to solidify a post and safeguard a lineage?" The weight of the realization settled on her. This wasn't just about her newfound immortality. This was about legacy, protection, and a deep, primordial bond that transcended time.

As intrigue filled her, a mix of emotions swirled within a heady combination of excitement, nervousness, and an undeniable draw toward understanding her role in this grand tapestry of magic and fate.

As the night deepened, a gust of wind made its way through the slightly opened window, causing the pages of the tome to flutter. The cool breeze caressed Itta's face, playing with stray strands of her hair, much like a lover's gentle touch. She closed her eyes, savoring the sensation, wondering if it was him, the creature, reaching out in this intimate manner.

"Are you here with me?" she whispered into the emptiness, feeling a bit audacious. The room, despite its vastness, suddenly felt close and intimate, as if it held the two of them —a woman and a guardian spirit. The Windswirled around her, enveloping her in its embrace, its touch unmistakably tender, making her heart race.

With a playful grin, Itta spoke aloud, "If I'm going to

help you, and us, you'll have to give me clearer signs, you know? A little less of the mysterious ambiance."

Almost in response, a single page in the tome flipped, pointing to a passage about the rites of bonding. Chuckling, she said, "Alright, point taken."

Itta leaned back in her chair, her fingers unconsciously tracing the edges of the tome. She felt connected, not just to the book, but to the whole mansion, the woods, and most profoundly, to the elusive guardian. She let herself revel in this connection, allowing the emotions, the sensations, and the energies to wash over her.

Deciding it was time to retire for the evening, she slowly rose from the plush armchair. She stretched her limbs, the soft fabric of her leggings hugging her body, accentuating her curves. With a mischievous glint in her eye, she exaggeratedly wiggled her hips, knowing, or at least hoping, that the guardian was watching.

The thought brought a flush to her cheeks and a playful smile to her lips. For all the seriousness of her mission, and the weight of her newfound responsibilities, there was an undeniable thrill in this flirtatious dance she was engaging in with the ethereal being.

Feeling a tad daring, she blew a teasing kiss toward the window. "Goodnight, guardian. Let's see what tomorrow brings."

And as she packed up for the night, heading to her room, she could swear she heard a faint, melodic whistle of the wind, like a lullaby, singing her to sleep. A promise of more revelations, deeper connections, and a journey like no other.

As Itta slept, the night felt thicker, pressing in on her with its weight. Her sheets tangled around her legs, sweat beading on her brow as her restless mind darted through the countless visions invading her slumber. Every revelation from the book, every whisper of the wind, and every intimate encounter with the guardian all raced through her dreams, painting a chaotic canvas of emotion, and understanding.

But then, like descending into a different layer of consciousness, everything shifted.

The weight of the night gave way, and she felt herself plummeting. A sensation so stark and sudden it robbed her breath, her heart drumming in her chest. When the free fall ceased, Itta found herself in an unfamiliar abyss.

The ground beneath her was slick and obsidian, reflecting her terrified expression back at her from every angle. Above, below, left, and right, there were countless iterations of herself, each mirroring the fear evident in her eyes. The depth and vastness of the place made her feel insignificant, a speck lost in an endless void.

The temperature rose, an oppressive heat intent on scorching away her very being. With every passing second, the heat became more stifling, her breaths coming in short, desperate gasps. Yet, for all the heat, no source of light was visible. The darkness was total and suffocating.

Then, a voice. Not the gentle, flirtatious wind-whispers of the guardian, but something colder, more menacing. It slithered around her, the words wrapping her in a cocoon of dread.

"Leave the Strange Mansion," it hissed, echoing in the

cavernous expanse. "You do not belong. What is unfolding will continue without you. The wheels are already in motion, and there is nothing you can do to stop them."

Every word was a knife, cutting into her spirit, seeding doubt and fear. Itta tried to shout, to question, to defend, but no sound emerged from her lips. She was voiceless, powerless, and utterly isolated in this nightmarish realm.

Suddenly, as swiftly as she had fallen into this place, she was jolted awake. Her body was slick with sweat, her sheets tangled around her, the morning light filtering in through the gaps in her curtains.

For a long moment, she lay there, trying to steady her racing heart, attempting to decipher the meaning of that malevolent dream. It was a stark contrast to the more sensual, enigmatic encounters she'd had before. Could this be a warning? A manifestation of her fears? Or a genuine threat?

Determination fueled her. It was evident now, more than ever, she needed answers. She had to meet her guardian, to truly understand her connection with him, and uncover the mystery unraveling around her. And she needed to *actually* meet him. Not in some fever dream that brought her pleasure.

Pushing off the sheets, Itta got up, her resolve firm. Today, she would seek out her ethereal protector, face the challenges head-on, and confront the shadowy threats that loomed. The Strange Mansion held secrets, and she was intent on unveiling them. No matter the cost.

Dear Aether,

The gravest fears I've harbored have swept into existence. Yesterday evening, as I lingered near Itta's window, watching over her, an unprecedented and bone-chilling squall disturbed me. She wasn't merely dreaming, Aether. She was being summoned, torn away from her realm, and thrust into the inferno of his dominion.

His name, as I'm sure you've surmised, is Fyrian, the Fire Guardian Protector. He has long lusted after our lands, our power, and now it seems, after our chosen ones. With Itta's arrival and her yet-to-be-realized potential, the temptation has become too great for him. Last night, he dared to touch her spirit, to transport her to the depths of his lair, aiming to intimidate her and ward her off.

I had long suspected his ambitions, his treacherous intentions, but now my suspicions are irrefutably confirmed. Fyrian wishes to weaken me, to frighten Itta away, and in doing so, leave our post vulnerable for his taking.

Anguish whipped through me as her body convulsed. The sheer panic knowing she was trapped in that fiery in-between, and I was powerless to intervene—it's a torment I cannot express in words. But I cannot and will not let this stand.

Aether, the sands in our hourglass are swiftly dwindling. We must act. The fates of our realms and the woman I'm irrevocably bound to are in peril.

In desperate hope,
Slyphor.

EIGHT

Before diving into another day of mysteries, Itta needed a proper meal. She couldn't survive on just sandwiches and fruit. And not just any meal—a feast fit for the soul, the kind she used to share with Sunday during their days of carefree childhood. The thought brought a smile to her face.

She needed to replenish her energy after the events of last night. Her brain was exploding with all the new information she was taking in and her body still sagged from the nightmare that had felt entirely too real. It wasn't a place her creature would've taken her. So, she needed to find him so she could figure out what she needed to do to stay safe.

She didn't know why she felt so possessive of the misty guardian, referring to him as "hers," but she reveled in the warmth that thought brought her. With a new spring in her step, Itta climbed the wide, ornate staircase leading to

Sunday's floor. She gave a light tap on the heavy wooden door.

Moments later, it swung open to reveal her cousin, her usually stoic face betraying a hint of surprise.

"I neeeeed some girl time," Itta started, eyes pleading. "You, me, brunch . . . mimosas?"

Sunday regarded her for a second, then with a single, succinct word, she agreed, "Fine."

Itta beamed, threading her arm through Sunday's, and playfully leading them both back downstairs. As they entered the grand kitchen, it was as if the mansion itself had antici-pated their needs. A rich spread was laid out on the large marble table: golden-brown French toast, crispy bacon, hash browns charred the way Itta loved, and vibrant bowls of freshly cut fruits.

Without a word, Sunday reached for a bottle of cham-pagne. The pop of the cork made Itta jump.

"Why so jumpy?" Sunday inquired, looking genuinely curious.

"Oh, it's . . ." Itta trailed off, deciding against sharing details of her unsettling dream. "Nothing, just lost in thought, I guess."

Sunday regarded her for a moment longer but let it go. They both turned and hoisted themselves up onto the edge of the counter, the cool marble cutting into the back of her thighs. They used to sit up here like this when they were younger, sharing snacks and secrets and it felt nice to be here again.

With plates piled high, they devoured the feast and

drained their glasses. Eventually running out of orange juice, they passed the champagne bottle between them, and Itta's mood improved.

"Hey." Itta hiccupped. "What's with all those files in your room? What are you working on?"

Sunday shrugged, never wanting to make anything a big deal. "It's old case files."

"For . . .?" Itta asked.

"I figured out that if I focus on a specific event or person I can guide my visions," Sunday replied. Itta knew that she'd been getting visions practically her entire life. Sometimes they were nonsensical and other times they predicted something that would happen in the future.

"So, I go through old unsolved case files to see if I can summon up a vision that can give me a clue or answer to the case," Sunday continued. "Then I send the information over to the correct division and hope they can do something with it."

Itta paused mid-sip. "Sunday! That's actually *incredibly* cool! Do you know if you've solved any yet?"

Sunday had a tiny glimmer in her eye that only someone who knew her really well would notice. "Yeah, I think I'm up to seventeen at this point," she said nonchalantly.

"OK, you are officially a badass. Cheers," Itta said as she raised her glass to clink against Sunday's.

The brunch and mimosas worked wonders, brightening Itta's spirit and mood, but the day was far from over. As she left Sunday to her unsolved mysteries, Itta decided it was time for a refreshing shower, to wash away the morning and fully awaken her senses.

She began the ascent up the grand staircase once more, her footsteps echoing in the stillness. Many rooms held countless memories, relics, and secrets, and one such secret hung upon a wall along the corridor leading to her bedroom —a grand tapestry that had been in the Strange Mansion for as long as anyone could remember.

The heavy wall hanging was an elaborate work of art, with vibrant threads of gold, silver, and a spectrum of colors interwoven to create a mesmerizing image. It showcased what Itta now knew as the guardians, the ones she had recently read about, but the detail was astonishing. It was incredible she'd walked past this countless times over the years and never thought to really study it.

Each guardian was depicted in their element—trees with deep roots and lush foliage for Earth, crashing waves and swirling pools for Water, and gusting winds carrying leaves and feathers for Wind. Seeing the blazing flames and embers for Fire made a chill run through Itta. Was that who she saw last night in her dream?

But what truly caught her attention were the eyes of these guardians. They seemed to shift, giving a lifelike quality to the figures. It was as though they were watching, waiting.

Suddenly, a faint movement on the tapestry made her blink. The woven guardians appeared to breathe, their forms subtly shifting. The trees of the Earth swayed, the waters of the sentinel rippled, the flames of the protector flickered, and the winds of the guardian stirred the fabric's fibers. The entire tapestry took on a spectral, dreamlike aura, making the room's temperature drop ever so slightly.

As she walked past it, the wall hanging came alive. It whispered to her, a gentle hum at first that soon turned into discernible words, uttered in an ancient, lilting tongue. Drawn like a moth to a flame, Itta stepped closer.

Suddenly, the tapestry whispered a phrase that resonated deep within her:

"Where the winds kiss the Earth, and Fire meets the sea, the guardian's heart shall be revealed to thee."

This next clue, a riddle meant for her, guided her onward on her quest. A new surge of energy coursed through Itta. It was a call to action, a directive she could not, would not, ignore.

She rushed to her room, her heart pounding with anticipation and excitement. Casting aside her brunch attire, she quickly stepped into the en suite bathroom, letting the warm spray of the shower wash over her. Every droplet felt like a new piece of understanding, a step closer to the enigma that awaited her.

Toweling off, she dressed in a comfortable outfit suitable for her outdoor quest. She tied her hair back, slipped into her boots, and with determination shining in her eyes, made her way outside, ready to continue her journey, to meet her destiny.

The brisk wind swept across Itta's face as she stepped into the tree line, an elemental caress whispering secrets of the ancient woods through the tendrils of her hair. The towering trees nodded a gentle welcome, their leaves rustling in a harmonious melody only she could understand. This symphony of nature enveloped her, their whispering tales of old magic and forgotten paths serenading her steps into the mystical unknown.

The woods transformed with every step she took; familiar, yet somehow new and enchanting. This wasn't the forest she knew from her childhood. This was something deeper, more primal, a realm where every leaf and twig vibrated with hidden energy, guiding her on a path destined by the unseen. Itta, her senses heightened, inhaled deeply, the sweet, Earthy scent of the forest grounding her, even as her heart fluttered with a mix of excitement and trepidation.

She thought about the tapestry, the flowing threads, and the soft whisper it gave her back at the mansion. It was a guide, a treasure map of sorts, but instead of leading her to gold, it drew her toward something infinitely more precious. Her thoughts twirled around the mysterious foggy creature from her visions and dreams; its essence lingered in the air, coaxing her deeper into the heart of the woods.

With every step, the tug in her belly grew stronger, a magnetic pull toward an unseen yet deeply felt presence. Itta listened to her intuition, weaving through the dense foliage, her steps instinctively guided by the gentle hum pulsating from the ground beneath her feet. As if the roots themselves knew of her mission, curving and entwining to forge a path, they led to answers shrouded in ancient mystery.

Her mind, aflutter with anticipation, pondered the myriad possibilities ahead. Would she meet the creature today? And if she did, what would that encounter be like? A warm sensation caressed her thoughts, a familiarity that soothed the edge of her nervous excitement. Her creature, her spectral guide, felt near, its essence a comforting embrace amidst the unknown.

Suddenly, a delicate whisper breezed through the trees, a soft, enthralling voice that beckoned her toward a dappled clearing ahead. Her heart raced, the enchanting sound an airy melody drawing her closer to her destiny. As she stepped into the light, her eyes widened in awe at the spectacular sight before her.

The dense canopy opened, revealing a vast expanse of verdant green. Lush grasses carpeted the floor, and wildflowers dotted the scenery, adding bursts of color to the emerald sea. Around the edges, ferns waved gently, and the dappled sunlight filtered through the swaying tree branches, casting playful, shifting patterns upon the ground. The air here was fragrant, a blend of fresh Earth, blooming flowers, and something deeper, an underlying hint of magic.

Dominating the serene beauty of the glade was the mesmerizing presence of her creature. He was a magnificent dance of colors, swirling and flowing, the very essence of the Windand magic made visible. His form shimmered with an iridescent hue, reflecting the sunlight in unpredictable, stunning patterns.

But as Itta approached, the ethereal form solidified. The once amorphous, misty figure molded itself, the gusts and whirls shaping into a defined structure. The gentle tendrils transformed into taut muscles and sinew. In moments, the Windand woods had morphed into a man, though still retaining the otherworldly grace and the slight hint of his misty origins at his edges.

Broad shoulders appeared, tapering into a chiseled torso, leading to a sight that made Itta gasp. Aside from his impossibly long, athletic legs that had him towering in the middle of the glade, Itta could also see he was *huge*. She sucked in a breath as her mind darted to dirty places of wondering what he would feel like between her hands or, even, her legs.

Itta could feel the soft hum of approval and laughter coming through her mind. She blushed as she finally pulled her eyes away from his cock. Itta took a few more confident steps toward the creature, took a deep breath, and lifted her head high.

Their gazes locked, and Itta found herself standing before a towering figure, an embodiment of both strength and gentleness. The creature, her guardian, her destiny, was no longer an elusive dream or an ethereal vision. He was real, tangible, and standing before her. The air was thick with anticipation, and a new chapter in Itta's mystical journey was about to begin.

NINE

"I *tta"*

The utterance of her name hung in the air, though no sound had passed through it. As if the creature, Slyphor, had spoken directly into her mind, his voice caressed her thoughts like a gentle breeze. Tentatively, she extended her arm, fingers outstretched, until they met the substance of his form.

Even solid as he appeared, his essence was still partly ethereal, and her fingers seemed to both touch and drift through him, a peculiar sensation that was neither solid nor mist. It was both startling and comforting in its strangeness.

"What's your name?" she inquired softly, her voice barely a whisper amidst the gentle rustle of the forest.

"Slyphor."

His answer was immediate, an affirmation delivered with the same thought-transcending communication.

"I am Slyphor, Guardian of the Ethereal Veil, Keeper of

the Woodland Echoes. My existence is bound to the preservation and balance of the energies within these woods and the mystical realms beyond our perception."

His voice resonated within her mind with a calm authority and gentle warmth soothing her apprehensions. Though his title held the weight of ancient traditions and untold secrets, his essence brushed against hers with a familiarity that transcended time.

"You, Itta, have walked within my shadows, slept within my embrace, and sought answers in my mysteries, Slyphor continued, a tender swirl of his unworldly form gently caressing her face. *Your lineage, your spirit, they are entwined with the magic of these woods, bound by threads of destiny that have woven through generations."*

And so, beneath the verdant canopy of the ancient, whispering woods, Itta and Slyphor stood, two beings brought together by a blend of fate and prophecies, on the brink of unraveling mysteries that had lain dormant for epochs. Together, they would navigate through the enshrouded paths of the unknown, where truths awaited to be discovered, and destinies were yet to be fulfilled.

Itta tilted her head back up at Slyphor and said, "I'm glad I have a name to call you now. I've been referring to you as 'my creature.'" She winced at her admission, hoping he wouldn't be offended by her choice of words.

But she felt a vibration of laughter through whatever shared bond they had. The warmth of his hands soothed her chilled skin as he wrapped his arms around her and tugged her closer. She could feel his impressive length press into her chest and settle between her breasts.

"Your creature. If I am yours, I will be called whatever you want."

"How can I see you? Touch you? Hear you?" Itta's eyes darted over his body, taking in all the details of his form.

The moment lingered, both curious and gentle, as Slyphor enveloped Itta in his airy embrace. He looked down at her, a visible serenity and kindness glowing within his eyes that captured the essence of the ancient woods around them.

"You perceive me, Itta, because your essence vibrates on the same frequency as mine," Slyphor began, his voice a soothing melody in her mind. *"Your ancestral lineage, the whispers of the forest that have always lingered in your ears, and the gentle tug of the magic that has guided you here—all are intertwined in a delicate, eternal dance. You are bound to the woods, to its energy, and to me because the blood that courses through your veins carries the ancient magic of the guardians."*

He tenderly lifted a strand of her hair, his form flickering between the muscular man before her and the swirling, misty entity she'd first encountered. *"You are both mortal and ethereal, a being who walks in two worlds. Your existence bridges the tangible reality you've always known and the unseen realms that have quietly shaped it."*

Itta absorbed his words, feeling them resonate deep within her soul, yet the mystery still cloaked her understanding in a gentle fog. "But why me? Why now? I've lived my whole life without knowing any of this . . ." her voice trailed off, a soft murmur amidst the eternal rustling of the forest.

Slyphor's eyes shimmered with a mixture of kindness and ancient wisdom. *"Destiny does not bow to the constraints of time, dear Itta. It weaves its tapestry in intricate, unpredictable patterns. Your soul has always been bound to this moment, even as you walked through life unaware of the strings of fate that gently guided your steps."*

He continued, *"The energies of these woods have long been guarded, kept in balance by the vigilant watch of beings like me. However, the veil that separates our worlds has begun to thin, and the magic that has slumbered quietly within your bloodline is now awakening, calling out to you to step forth and embrace your role."*

Itta felt a mix of fascination and a daunting sense of responsibility intertwining within her. Slyphor, this creature of both solidity and mist, of both the now and the eternal, was offering answers, yet each revelation led to more questions cascading through her mind.

With her voice barely above a whisper, she asked, "What is this role you speak of, Slyphor? What mission have I been given?"

In the silent communion amidst the trees, Slyphor shared the tales of the past, the guardians who once walked where Itta now stood, and the delicate balance that kept the magic of the woods in harmonious flow. It was a journey into the unknown, a path Itta was destined to walk, yet one that she would not have to traverse alone.

"Walk with me, Itta," Slyphor's voice invited, extending a hand that was at once solid and somehow insubstantial.

As she took his hand, they strolled through the enchanted forest, their steps in a delicate dance with the whispering of the leaves above. Slyphor led her to places where the magic of the woods shimmered visibly in the air— places where vibrant flowers bloomed out of season and where trees seemed to breathe with an ancient, knowing rhythm.

With every step, every sight, Slyphor shared tales of the eons he'd witnessed, of the creatures, both gentle and fierce, that had tread upon the ground they now walked. And in his eyes, an inexplicable depth sparkled, hinting at untold stories and unseen worlds.

In between his tales of guardians and mystical realms, he'd throw her gentle, inquisitive glances, making playful, flirty remarks that brought a soft blush to Itta's cheeks. And as they walked, Itta had to train her eyes forward, the gently sway of his length distracting her a few times.

"You carry the wild beauty of these woods in your eyes, Itta," he commented softly, his voice a gentle caress against her thoughts.

She smirked slightly, trying to navigate the flurry of emotions his presence stirred within her. "Are all mystical forest entities such charmers, or is it just you?"

He laughed, a rich, warm sound carried away by the breeze, and for a moment, they locked eyes, an unspoken understanding passing between them. But then, with an affectionate smile, he simply continued to lead her through his timeless world.

After a few moments of silence, where the harmonious whispers of the forest around them filled the air, Itta, with a sly, teasing smile playing at the corners of her lips, turned her gaze toward Slyphor. "Do you ever . . . watch me, back at the mansion?" Her eyes glimmered with playful curiosity, her voice a gentle, flirty murmur in the growing dusk.

Slyphor, taken aback by her boldness but amused by her inquisitive nature, let a secretive, yet charming smile dance across his ethereal face. His form flickered with a cascade of vibrant, enchanting colors as he pondered his response.

"I may have been known to drift through the realms from time to time," he responded with a twinkle of mischief in his eyes, *"ensuring the safety of those who dwell within the boundaries of my forest, my domain. Sometimes, that protective gaze may wander to the mansion, to you. After all, ensuring your safety, lovely Itta, is ensuring the safety of this ancient, enchanted place."*

Itta's heart fluttered, a soft warmth spreading through her at his veiled confession. "So, all those times I felt a strange chill, a peculiar presence, that was you, wasn't it?" she pressed gently, her voice soft and laced with a delicate, teasing tone. "My unseen, mystical guardian."

Slyphor's gaze softened, the vibrant colors swirling within his form becoming a gentle, caressing mist. *"Guilty as charged,"* he confessed, his voice a tender murmur that intertwined with the soft rustling of the leaves overhead. *"You captivate me, Itta. The way you move through your world and dance at the edge of mine . . . it is its own type of magic."*

As the sun began its descent, casting long shadows upon the forest floor, Slyphor conjured a quaint, secluded spot for them to rest. With a graceful wave of his hand, a cascade of luminous flowers blossomed around, forming a serene, enchanting haven.

Itta settled amidst the radiant blooms, and although Slyphor didn't require sustenance, he watched attentively, his gaze gentle and admiring, as she nibbled on the provisions she'd brought. His company, his very existence, it all seemed like a vivid, beautiful dream from which she never wished to wake.

As twilight draped the woods in hues of lavender and soft pink, Slyphor spoke of the loneliness eternity had etched into his existence, of the longing for a companion, a mate to share in the boundless epochs stretching out before him.

"I have lingered in this existence, safeguarding the equilibrium of energies, watching generations of your ancestors live their brief, fervent lives," he confessed, a tangible vulnerability underscoring his words. *"Yet, there lies a vacancy within me, an emptiness that echoes through the centuries. Guardians of my kind find completeness, a harmonizing of energies, with a chosen mate."*

Itta, absorbing his words, felt a strange, compelling pull in his direction, a desire to step into his eternal world and soothe the solitude that veiled his essence. Yet, she held back, her mortal hesitations whispering uncertainties into her heart.

As the day drew to its close and Itta's mortal frame grew weary, Slyphor, with a tenderness that seemed to transcend time, lifted her into his arms. His form, a mesmerizing blend of solidity and mist, held her securely as they moved through the woods, toward the edge where her two worlds met.

"Where will you go now?" Itta asked as Slyphor sat her gently back on the Earth.

"I need to border the edges of the realm. There have been .. . attempts from other guardians to take over my post."

Itta's face scrunched up in concern at this bit of information. "Will you be safe?"

"You are concerned for my safety?"

"I don't want you to get hurt," Itta confessed.

"I promise I will stay unharmed. For you."

Itta yawned.

"It is time for you to rest now. Go inside. We will see each other again."

"Will you come visit me again? In my dreams, I mean." She blushed as she realized the implications of her request. For when Slyphor had visited her in her dreams it had been solely for her pleasure.

Slyphor smiled down at her as he pushed her hair back over her shoulders. *"I would risk everything just for another chance to watch you come undone for me, Itta."*

With a final glance up at Slyphor, where Itta did take note of the swell of his length, she gently pulled away, her fingers lingering on the cool, misty form of Slyphor. Her heart fluttered in her chest, carrying a weight of emotions she could not yet decipher. With a soft, reluctant smile, she whispered, "Goodbye, for now, my creature."

As she turned away, moving toward the mansion, her mind swirled with thoughts of the enchanted forest, the whispered secrets, and the hauntingly beautiful being that had woven himself into the tapestry of her destiny. Itta found herself suspended between two worlds, each calling to her in different, irresistible melodies.

Slyphor's words, the tender look in his ephemeral eyes, lingered in her mind, tugging at her heartstrings. She was drawn into a mystery that spanned through time, and as she approached the mansion, an unexpected resolve settled within her. She would navigate through this mesmerizing enigma, exploring the depths of the ancient magic, and perhaps, uncover the secrets that bound her fate to the mystical guardian of the woods.

Dear Aether,

In the shadows of the ancient, whispering trees, I encountered her—Itta, the one whose lineage pulses with the unbroken magic that has so long guarded these hallowed woods. Her presence is an enigma, simultaneously delicate and formidable, a duality of fragility and strength I have not witnessed in eons.

I beheld her, her long, cascading blonde hair shimmering like streams of liquid gold under the celestial moonlight. Her form, adorned with curves generous and inviting, held a grace that belied the sheer force of her innate power. Her skin, as smooth as the tranquil surfaces of our sacred forest pools, was kissed by the gentle moon, casting her in a soft, ethereal glow.

It's challenging, Aether, to describe the torrent of emotions that cascade through me, a being who has existed for time immemorial, unyielding, and untouched by such mortal affections. Yet, here I find myself, profoundly moved, bound by a yearning to shield her, to protect her from any peril that might dare tread upon her path.

In her eyes, I glimpsed a spirit untamed and unburdened by the ravages of our eternal struggle. Her innocence, untainted by the shadows that have so often threatened these sacred groves, fills me with both admiration and trepidation. My essence intertwines with a fervent wish: that she may remain untouched by the darkness that looms on our horizon.

Yet, herein lies my internal tempest, dear Aether, for while my being surges with a desire to envelop her in a sanctuary free from our eternal conflict, I recognize the essence of her destiny. It's a role that demands of her strength and sacrifices I wish she could be spared from.

I long to stand beside her, to be her steadfast guardian as she navigates the treacherous paths that await. Yet, an undying fear courses through me, pondering the readiness of her spirit to accept and ascend into the role fate has so cruelly thrust upon her.

The mortal realm, with its fleeting joys and

inevitable sorrows, is a sphere I observe yet seldom touch. But through Itta, I have felt the tender, aching beauty of their transient existence. Her presence, in its gentle, unassuming manner, has pierced through the veils of my eternal solitude, drawing forth a love I had not believed myself capable of harboring.

Is this what it means to fear, Aether? To be entwined so deeply with a soul that the mere thought of their suffering or demise brings forth a torrent of despair? I am bound by my duty, as is she, yet I find my resolve shaken by this newfound vulnerability.

What shall become of us, ancient friend? In these woods, where our essences observe the ceaseless march of time, I find myself pondering the future with a cautious optimism and an unspoken dread.

With the silent whispers of the eternal forest,

Slyphor

The mansion, vast and enigmatic, echoed with the unspoken tales of the ages as Itta nestled into the embracing solitude of the library, its musty pages whispering secrets of the guardians and the ancient magic they sheltered. Three nights had meandered by since her enchanting encounter with Slyphor in the depths of the forest.

She found herself submerged in anticipation, awash with a fusion of emotions—wonder, exhilaration, and an undeniable undercurrent of anxiety. Her nights were restless, punctuated by dreams in which shadows loomed and flickers of Slyphor's formless visage weaved in and out of her slumber.

The Elemental Guardians, she'd learned, were eternal beings, each bound to a natural element and charged with the preservation and balance of the magic within their respective realms. Slyphor, a guardian of wind, was her lineage's protector, a spectral sentinel safeguarding the secrets and

mystical potency of her family throughout countless generations. His role was vital, ensuring the perpetual flow of magic
through nature, sustaining both the Earthly and ethereal in
harmonious balance.

But Slyphor's presence had suggested the emergence of a
tempest unseen. His elemental counterparts, notably the one
bound to the inferno's wrath and unyielding blaze, threatened the ageless equilibrium, harboring intentions that
remained shrouded in mystery and menace. The Elemental
Guardians, in their respective domains, were to exist in unity,
each granting and drawing power in a cycle unbroken, yet
these veiled threats whispered of discord amongst the eternal.

Itta found her thoughts spiraling amidst the questions
that lingered in the aftermath of the revelations. The
guardians held their posts, yet Slyphor spoke of his position
teetering on a precipice, a discord woven by the flames of
rebellion. Was it indeed the Fire Guardian that sought to
usurp, to dismantle the perennial balance that had sustained
their magic for so long?

The texts spoke of the importance of guardianship and
rejuvenation of the magic; an element, when neglected or
usurped, could spell disaster for both the guardians and those
they protected. The elemental balance was not merely a prin-
ciple—it was a necessity. The realms of elements, when
skewed, could release chaos, affecting not merely the spectral
beings but cascading into the mortal world with a fury
unfettered.

With her lineage intrinsically linked to the guardians, Itta
pondered the depth of her role in this timeless battle. What

did it mean to shield her lineage, and by extension, the world, from the cascade of an elemental imbalance? If she were to falter, to fail in understanding and wielding her newfound role and the powers it entailed, what would become of the worlds that hovered in the fragile balance?

As her eyes meandered over the ancient script, seeking answers in the shadows of the words left behind by her ancestors, she felt the soft, ephemeral brush of a familiar presence weaving through her consciousness. Her heart fluttered, and for a moment, the questions cloaking her in their ponderous weight dissipated, replaced by an inexplicable calm and a connection that transcended time.

Slyphor. His name whispered through her spirit, an unspoken promise, a delicate tether binding them amidst the chaos that swirled unseen. And she found herself, once more, drawn into the ethereal embrace of dreams, where answers and enigmas wove into the tapestry of their unfolding destiny.

Itta sensed the gentle caress of a plush rug beneath her as she was tenderly lowered down. The crackling warmth of a vibrant Fire greeted her, its lively flames casting a mesmerizing, flickering glow around the room.

The mansion slumbered deeply in nocturnal stillness, yet within the library, an energetic fervor quietly stirred. Itta's smile blossomed gently upon sensing Slyphor's familiar presence enveloping her. Glimmers of his iridescent form tantalizingly wove through the air, gradually morphing into his distinctive, mystical shape around her.

Itta wanted to play. She used her hands to roam over her

own body while she locked eyes with Slyphor. His midnight blue gaze deepened as Itta slipped her loose t-shirt and shorts off, leaving her bare on the rug before him.

His iridescent form flashed shades of purples and blues as he hovered over Itta. She wanted to see how far she could take it with him. After all the unknown and uncertainty the last few days had brought her, she wanted to take back some control.

Itta brought her knees up and widened her legs, trailing a hand down to her inner thighs. With her other hand she cupped a handful of her breasts and rubbed, reaching for her nipple, and pinching slightly.

"I love watching you touch yourself, Itta."

Itta smiled at Slyphor as he hovered close. She wanted to feel him. She wanted him to grip her and claim her.

"You aren't ready for that, my love."

Itta groaned and Slyphor chuckled.

"You'll need to be prepared for it. And I'll want you in my clearing so I can fully unleash with you. I must keep ahold of my magic too much while I'm here."

Itta was disappointed but thrilled at the same time. It wouldn't be happening tonight, but Slyphor did want it to happen. And she wanted it too. She didn't fully understand it but there was this magnetic connection between her and Slyphor getting stronger by the day. And the stronger that connection got, the stronger her needs became. She wasn't sure how much longer her body could wait.

"Are you wet for me?"

"Why don't you come find out for yourself?" Itta asked

as she trailed one finger down her middle, inwardly hissing at the contact. Pleasure had never felt like this for her before. One thought about Slyphor, one look from him, one miniscule feel of his presence and she would practically come undone.

Slyphor's form shifted slightly and soon Itta could feel hands grip and squeeze her waist. Those hands slid up and cupped her breasts, tweaking both nipples sharply.

"Do you trust me?"

Itta replied without an ounce of hesitation, "Yes."

Without removing his hands from her breasts, Slyphor shifted once more. An additional hand formed from his mist and Itta gasped as one of its fingers slid in between her folds.

"Do I scare you?"

"No," Itta whispered, "Please, I want more."

Slyphor smiled down at her, his eyes dark as he thickened his finger and shoved it deeper. Itta could feel and hear her wetness coating him. She wasn't ashamed or embarrassed. She wanted to give him more.

Itta sat up slightly. She wanted to watch him as he ravaged her. She peered down between her legs and was mesmerized by the sight of him. A thick finger, slightly thinner than a regular cock slid into her. The tip of the finger had ridges Itta could feel brush against her insides as Slyphor fucked her with it.

His other hands roamed her body, caressing her breasts, gripping her chin, pushing back her hair. It was as if all Slyphor wanted to do was touch her, explore her. And she loved it. Itta leaned back on her elbows and tilted her chin to the ceiling as his finger continued stretching her. It pulsed and heated up as it settled deep in her.

Itta bounced and ground herself into his hand. She was close.

"Oh, fuck me, oh god. More. Can you give me more?" Itta was a fiend for pleasure.

"I will give you whatever you want, Itta."

Slyphor thickened the finger inside her, pounding it in deeper and deeper. He used another hand to rub circles on her clit and he used another to softly grip her neck. With slight pressure around her throat, Slyphor pinched her clit and shoved his finger deeper inside her.

Itta's legs tightened and shook, her toes curling in tightly. The waves of her orgasm came out in a force. She whimpered and gasped as she soaked his hand. Her muscles flexed around the finger inside her and the shockwaves were sensitive as he slowly slid it in and out as she came down from her high.

"Oh my god," Itta said with a ragged breath. "That was . . ."

"Beautiful. You are the most beautiful thing I've ever gotten the pleasure of seeing."

Itta smiled lazily as Slyphor removed himself from her. Her eyes were glazed, her cheeks flushed. If the rug had been more comfortable, she probably could've slept there all night. But Slyphor knew.

He scooped her up and tucked her into his arms as he gathered her close and led her upstairs to her room. If anyone had come out, Itta wondered what they would've seen.

Slyphor made it to her room and pushed open her door, laying her gently on the bed.

She rolled over and tried to reach for him. She could see he was impossibly hard. His cock heavy in between his legs.

"Please, let me," she said. She wanted to return the favor.

"It is okay, my love, you are not ready. There are things we need to go over first."

"I know that you're big. I can take it," Itta replied, eyes treacherously closing.

Slyphor chuckled. *"It's not just that. There are implications of us . . . being together in that way. We will talk about it later. Sleep, my love."*

Itta lay quietly, the soft fabric of her bed linens gently cradling her, a stark contrast to the fervor of moments ago. Her mind, though foggy from the heady mix of emotions and the remnant echoes of Slyphor's presence, fluttered with reflections. Her fingers lightly traced the spots on her body where moments ago, a unique connection was formed— both mystical and visceral, yet not entirely Earthly.

She thought back to how his ethereal touch had felt, that paradox of tangible yet incorporeal, somehow warm and chilling all at once. He'd been a swirl of comforting tenderness and puzzling distance, a creature that was hers yet remained partly out of grasp. They had shared a gentle, meaningful connection, dancing on the delicate edge of something deeper, something that might bridge their two worlds in a way neither of them fully understood.

As her eyelids began to weigh heavily with impending sleep, she found her thoughts weaving through the tapestry of information she'd absorbed over the past few days. The guardians, each an embodiment of an elemental force, had overseen the magic for millennia, ensuring the balance of energies and safeguarding the lineage of those entwined with their destiny. Slyphor, the Guardian of the Wind, had been her family's protector, a watcher over their magical history, gently guiding and, where needed, intervening across the ages.

She considered his unspoken vulnerability, his nebulous fears that rippled beneath his composed exterior. There had been an edge of desperation to his touch, an unspoken plea which transcended words. She replayed their conversation, how he'd alluded to threats to his guardianship, the ominous specter of the Fire Elemental Guardian permeating the edges of her thoughts.

As her mind drifted between wakefulness and the allure of sleep, she pondered what her role truly entailed. To protect her lineage, to safeguard the magic—it all felt so overwhelmingly intangible, as transient as Slyphor's misty form. Her mind wrestled with understanding what was truly at stake. What would her failure mean for her family, for their history, and their future?

Her thoughts spiraled, dovetailing into memories of her ancestors, whose portraits adorned the mansion with eyes that held tales of epochs gone by. Was it their approval she sensed in the dusty, stoic air of the manor, or was it an urging to correct a path that had somehow gone awry? Her role as the chosen one was still shrouded in mystery, an enigma that seemed increasingly daunting as the nights wore on.

Eventually, her turbulent musings began to ebb, giving way to a sea of tranquil drowsiness. Her mind, though fraught with questions and dilemmas, loosened its tight coil, floating into a gentle, dream-infused sleep.

In her dreams, there was a comforting whisper of winds, a soft, reassuring touch that felt like Slyphor's lingering presence. It enwrapped her in a gentle embrace, tugging her toward a realm where answers might be found, where the whisper of ancient truths might eventually be understood.

As she journeyed through this ethereal dreamscape, a soft light appeared, hinting at revelations yet to be unveiled. It was here, suspended between the tangible world and the abyss of the unknown, that Itta might yet find the keys to unlock her destiny, to comprehend her role in a story that spanned both time and the cosmos.

In the embrace of slumber, she drifted, somewhere between the legacy of the past and the unknown journey ahead, enshrouded by the loving gusts of a guardian, who, from the shadows, vowed an eternal, protective watch over her.

TWELVE

Days flowed into one another, autumn's vivid palette gradually muted by the encroaching fingers of winter. Itta, while engrossed in her studies, felt the omnipresent void of Slyphor's absence, his lingering whispers a bittersweet melody in the recesses of her mind. Her days were marked by a peculiar loneliness, punctuated by the vibrant, albeit spectral, memory of Slyphor's touch and the soulful depth of his presence.

As the first snowflakes descended, gently dusting the world in a hushed blanket of white, Itta often found herself gazing out the window, her thoughts meandering through the intricate tapestry of fate, destiny, and the ephemeral caress of a love as ancient as it was new. The looming Winter Solstice, traditionally a time of celebration and unity in her family, now held an unspoken tension, an invisible thread tying her to a destiny still shrouded in mystery.

The mansion, despite its stoic permanence, echoed with

a silent anticipation, its hallways whispering secrets of the past, and perhaps, foresights of the future. Itta, while preparing for the Solstice festivities, couldn't shake the feeling that the threads of time were converging, weaving toward a pivotal moment that seemed just out of reach.

She was startled one crisp winter evening by the sudden appearance of an elegantly scribed letter on her desk. Its presence was unexpected, its origin inexplicable. Her name, written with a graceful flourish, beckoned her to unveil its contents.

Itta's hands, steady yet tentative, unfolded the parchment, revealing the words of Aether, an entity known to her through lore and the murmurings of Slyphor.

Dearest Itta,

May this letter find you in good health and spirits despite the mysteries that have recently enveloped your path. My name is Aether, a guardian of realms and a close confidante to Slyphor, whom you have come to know quite intimately. It is rare, if not unprecedented, for our kind to communicate so directly with those we safeguard, yet the threads of destiny have woven a tale that necessitates exception.

I pen this correspondence with dual intentions: to shed light upon the obscurities you face and to share a concealed truth that significantly concerns both you and our ethereal friend. Slyphor has grappled with a profound internal struggle, torn between his deeply rooted feelings for you and the duty to allow you an uninfluenced journey toward self-discovery. His physical absence, although laden with emotional hardship, is a testa-

ment to the immense respect and genuine love he harbors for you.

There exists a delicate equilibrium upon which our guardianship and the welfare of your lineage precariously perch. The bond between you and Slyphor, particularly its formal acknowledgment and consummation, must be solidified before the arrival of this Winter Solstice, else our ethereal comrade's position as Guardian falls into perilous jeopardy. The fervor and ambition of a rival elemental guardian, of the fiery persuasion, threaten to usurp Slyphor's stance, thereby endangering the protective enchantments that have shielded the women of your lineage for eons.

Should such a catastrophic event transpire, wherein Slyphor is dethroned from his post, the once-immortal souls of countless women, both ancestral and descendent, within your lineage would be rendered mortal. The demise of such enchantments implies an imminent and widespread perish, and it is with a heavy heart that I reveal this grievous potentiality.

In sharing these words, I must emphasize that your autonomy and freedom will remain paramount in our respects and intentions. Thus, despite the urgency and severity of the circumstances at hand, the decision, dear Itta, remains intrinsically yours to make. Whether it be a path toward unbridled love, selfless sacrifice, or an alternative yet unseen, may you find tranquility and conviction in whatever choice you deem fit.

I extend to you the sincerest wishes of strength and clarity amidst the tempest of dilemmas you now face and remain an *ally, albeit from the shadows, in whatever journey you embark upon.*

With Utmost Respect,

Aether

The parchment slipped from Itta's fingers, softly cascading to the wooden floor with a gentleness that sharply contrasted the turmoil now churning within her. Her hands, tremoring slightly, hovered in the space where the letter had been, a whisper of motion barely visible yet incredibly potent in its fragility.

In the quiet sanctuary of her room, Itta's breath caught, trapped within the confines of her throat as the magnitude of Aether's words sank in. A myriad of emotions swirled within her, a maelstrom of love, duty, fear, and disbelief that threatened to consume her utterly. Her heart, which once beat rhythmically with the gentle ebb and flow of her everyday worries and joys, now thundered erratically against her ribcage, a frantic and desperate creature pleading for release.

Itta staggered backward, her back finding the support of the cool, sturdy wall. Her mind, a once-organized collection of reason and practicality, spiraled into chaos as she grappled with the reality now laid so mercilessly before her. The coolness of the wall seeped through her gown, an incongruous sensation that oddly grounded her in the midst of her internal tempest.

How had everything come to this point? The beautiful, ephemeral moments shared with Slyphor in the realm of both dreams and reality had felt so pure, so genuine. His touch, his voice, the intensity of his gaze—was it all rooted in the desperation of an unspoken duty, a silent plea concealed behind those soulful eyes?

"No . . ." Itta whispered into the space, her voice a mere shadow amidst the encroaching dread. "He loves me. I felt it. It was . . . real."

Memories of her time with Slyphor flickered across her mind's eye, each tender touch and shared glance acting as both a salve to her burgeoning panic and a blade to her already fraying composure. A tear trailed down her cheek, catching the soft glow of the moonlight filtering through her window, its path a testament to the pain coursing through her veins.

She sank to the floor, her legs folding beneath her as sobs quietly shook her frame. The letter, still poised delicately beside her, radiated an aura of solemnity, a tangible reminder of the dire straits her lineage now faced. Each word pulsed with urgency, yet also a strange kind of respect for her autonomy and emotion.

A part of her wanted to rail against the circumstances, to reject the weighty mantle now thrust upon her shoulders. But amidst the tumult of her emotions, a spark of determination, minute yet unyielding, kindled within the depths of her soul.

Could she turn away from this path, knowing the consequences of such a decision? Was her love for Slyphor potent enough to tether him to his post, to protect countless souls from a cataclysmic fate? Only time, it seemed, would unveil the answers to such heart-wrenching dilemmas.

In the muted tranquility following Aether's revelatory

letter, something else caught Itta's eye: a delicate glint emanating from within the now-crumpled parchment. Cautiously, with hands still trembling from the emotional tempest, she retrieved a small, ornate locket that had silently spilled onto the floor, its presence an unnoticed whisper amidst her internal turmoil.

The locket was exquisitely crafted, wrought from an unknown metal that shimmered with an ethereal glow, akin to the gentle luminescence of Slyphor's presence. It was at once foreign and familiar, its surface etched with patterns that danced and shifted as she turned it gently within her fingers. The design whispered tales of ancient power and secret knowledge, spirals interweaving with delicate symbols that pulsed with a latent energy.

Tentatively, Itta opened the locket. Inside, a miniature painting of a woman gazed back at her. The resemblance was uncanny: She could see herself in the gentle curve of the woman's cheek, the fierce determination in her eyes, and yet, there were subtle differences, a timeless quality that spoke of another era, another life. It was as if she was peering across the centuries into a mirror of her own soul, reflected through the lineage of women who had come before her.

Tears welled anew in her eyes, but this time they were tinged with a different emotion—a combination of gratitude and an awakening understanding. This woman, whoever she was, had faced her own trials, her own impossible decisions, and yet her gaze spoke of strength, compassion, and a love that had clearly endured beyond the temporal confines of her Earthly existence.

A soft sigh escaped Itta's lips as she clutched the locket to her heart, feeling a strange warmth emanating from the delicate artifact. Her mind raced with the stories it might tell, the truths it might hold, and the wisdom it might impart. Somehow, the locket felt like a beacon, an ancestral guide affirming her importance in a tapestry woven through time, love, and sacrifice.

Her thoughts wandered to the woman in the locket, to Slyphor, and to the countless women whose fates were now inexplicably intertwined with her own. A calm determination replaced the frenzied tumult within her, a resolve forged from the unbroken chain of strength, endurance, and unyielding love that now linked them together across the eons.

She knew, in that crystalline moment, she was not alone in this. The locket was a tangible reminder of the power and resilience of her lineage, of the guardians who had silently protected them, and of the love that had endured through every trial and tribulation. It was a legacy of women who had faced the unthinkable and had emerged from the abyss, their spirits unbroken and their love unextinguished.

Slowly, Itta rose from the floor, the locket clasped tightly in her hand. Her eyes, reflecting the undying flame of generations of fearless women, gazed out of the window, where the first snow of winter danced whimsically through the air. The path ahead was fraught with uncertainty, shrouded in mystery and danger, and yet she would walk it unflinchingly, with the strength of her ancestors coursing through her veins and their whispers guiding her way.

Whatever the future held, she would meet it with a heart unburdened by fear and a soul fortified by an eternal, unbreakable love. And so, with the locket securely around her neck, a symbol of timeless strength and unity, Itta stepped forward into the unknown, ready to forge her own link in the everlasting chain of their shared destiny.

Aether,

Your audacity cuts through my essence, slicing through the core of the delicate equilibrium I meticulously tried to maintain with Itta. An incensed inferno blazes within me, fueled by the untold implications of your unsolicited intervention.

How dare you! My bond with Itta, the love we share, it's sacred, intimate—a sanctuary away from the exacting eyes of otherworldly beings like us. It is a relationship unadulterated by the knowledge of cosmic plights and the inherent dangers posed by our ethereal kindred. To violate this sanctuary with the truths I sought to shield her from is a transgression of unspeakable proportions.

Your letter, while crafted with eloquent care, heaved upon her a burden I desperately wished to spare her from. She was never meant to be thrust into the maelstrom of our celestial dilemmas, forced to grapple with the precarious fate of the guardians and the mortals intertwined. You unloaded a weight upon her shoulders that I would have willingly borne alone, if only to preserve the untainted sparkle in her eyes.

As my initial fury simmers, however, a reluctant acknowledgement of the potential necessity of your actions begins to weave through the tempest of my emotions. I must begrudgingly concede that your intrusion, while disruptive and unbidden, may harbor an unintended wisdom. In your interference, you have unwillingly provided a mirror to my own failings, my cowardice in keeping the truth shrouded from her sight.

I feel her now more than ever, Aether—her pain, her resolution, the embodiment of strength that burgeons within her soul despite the hurricane of revelations you have unleashed. Her vitality, even amidst the chaos, breathes a new life into the bond that tethers our beings. The connection sears through me, a blazing testament to her unspoken resolve and the unbreakable ties binding us through realms.

If I am to salvage an inkling of respect for you, Aether, I must believe your actions were not sprouted from a place of malevolence or control, but from a genuine, if misguidedly paternal, concern. My fervent hope is that the turbulence you've set into motion will cascade toward a future where Itta emerges not as a victim of our celestial machinations, but as a beacon of unyielding strength and autonomy.

In an abyss of confusion and irate dismay,
Slyphor

FOURTEEN

With days remaining before the longest night of the year and her family's Winter Solstice celebrations, Itta needed to act quickly. With purposeful strides, she ventured into the mysterious allure of the ethereal glade, a place where the veils between realms seemed tantalizingly thin, where the essence of Slyphor had once danced most vibrantly within the Earthly confines.

Her heart fluttered, an enchanting blend of anticipation and serene resolve enveloping her soul as she treaded through the dappled moonlight, fingers gently caressing the cool, whispered blessings of the night.

In her arms, she cradled elements sacred and ancient, passed down through the whispered wisdom of generations and solidified through the pages of aged texts. Her ancestors had spoken of the ritual, a union of elemental homage and the tangible devotion of intertwined souls.

She had pored over the pages of the traditional ritual, taking meticulous notes. She didn't want to get one element wrong for fear it would weaken the bond she hoped to create. She was ready. For her ancestors. For love. For *her creature*. She would do this.

Itta turned the Crystal of Purity, a beacon meant to signal her unwavering intent through the veiled realms, in her palm. It gleamed brilliantly, refracting the moonlight into a myriad of splendid hues across the forest floor. With gentleness, she placed it at the northernmost point of a circle she envisioned within the glade, whispering ancient words that breathed a celestial light into the crystal.

To the south, she gingerly placed a Flame of Eternal Bond, its undying Fire symbolizing the perpetual unity of their souls, an unbreakable connection destined to traverse time and space. As the flame flickered into existence, its warmth kissed her skin, a comforting caress amidst the cool embrace of the night.

To the east, she suspended the Feather of Ethereal Paths, its iridescence shimmering with the promises of journeys yet untold, a guide through the celestial realms that awaited their entwined fates. It floated gently, suspended in an unseen breeze, tethered to the energies swirling within the glade.

Lastly, to the west, she placed the Chalice of Endless Waters, filled with water drawn from the Enchanted Spring, a tribute to the undulating tides of emotions and the depth of their boundless love.

At the center, she gently unfurled a delicate Silken Veil, a manifestation of vulnerability, trust, and the gentle embrace of forthcoming unions. Her fingers traced its softness, a silent prayer cascading from her lips as she shed her warm layers and enveloped herself within its translucent folds.

Each element, symbolic and potent, created a harmonic convergence within the glade, an inviting melody meant to summon Slyphor to the Earthly realm, to the precipice of their shared destiny. Itta, adorned in a diaphanous veil of celestial white, stepped into the center, her heart a rhythmic serenade inviting him into the sacred space she'd conjured.

Her voice, soft yet unwavering, whispered through the glade, a verbal tether reaching through the realms toward him. "Slyphor, my love, my eternal flame, I summon thee to this Earthly plane. With elements ancient and intentions pure, I beckon thee to join me, our destinies to secure."

The glade, bathed in the gentle glow of the ritualistic elements, pulsed with an expectant energy, the world holding its breath in tantalizing anticipation of the union. Itta, her heart ablaze with love and tranquil determination, waited amidst the enchanted circle, her spirit calling out to him across the expanse of existence, inviting him into a future penned by their own hands.

She waited, the silence of the glade enveloping her like a gentle embrace, her soul, bright and resolute, reaching out toward the shadowed realms, toward the being whose essence had become inextricably woven with her own. And in that sacred, suspended moment, the universe seemed to bow in respect to their love, to the fated confluence of mortal and ethereal, of destinies delicately entwined through the bound-less tapestry of time.

So, in the glade, where realms intertwined and fates were birthed amidst the whispered secrets of the universe, Itta stood, a beacon of love, strength, and willing sacrifice, ready to step forward into the unwritten chapters of their shared eternity.

Suddenly, the air quivered, a palpable tension pulling at the threads of the enchanting tableau before erupting into a vortex of raw, pulsating energy. From the abyss of realms unseen, Slyphor emerged, a storm of turbulent emotions wrapped in a graceful visage of celestial beauty and haunting sorrow.

He didn't approach as one might expect of a lover, but rather as a tempest, a whirlwind of chaotic energy, swirling around her, the gusts of his passage riffling through the silken veil and tossing her blonde curls into a frenetic dance. His voice, once a tender caress, now rumbled with the echoes of distant thunder, eyes ablaze with an infernal mixture of torment and insatiable desire.

"Itta . . . is this truly your desire? To chain your essence to mine in eternal synchrony, your mortal coil forever bound to the undying flame of our entwining destinies?" His words, though whispered, emanated from the core of the universe, vibrating with a power that stilled the heartbeat of the world.

She, undeterred by the commotion that enveloped her, anchored her gaze upon him, an unwavering resolve alit within her verdant eyes. "It is, Slyphor. My heart, my soul, they call for you across the eons, tethering me to you with bonds unbreakable and fervently sought."

A silence, punctuated only by the restless rustling of the ancient trees, enveloped the glade as Slyphor stilled, his turbulent energies momentarily quelled by her assertion. Slowly, the tempest subsided, his form materializing before her, eyes locked onto hers, a myriad of unspoken pleas lingering within their indigo depths.

He stepped forward, the ethereal distance between them seeming to stretch and contract in a disorienting dance, until his form, solid yet inexplicably otherworldly, stood mere breaths away from her. His voice, a gentle caress yet laden with a haunting gravity, whispered into the infinite space between them.

"There's more you must know, beloved, a truth that dwells within the shadows of this eternal pledge." His hand, a gentle wraith, caressed the air near her cheek, aching for contact yet restrained by the revelations yet unspoken. *"If you proceed, if our souls entwine in an immortal embrace, you will be bound to this place, to the locus of our union, for all of eternity."*

He paused, eyes searching hers for any flicker of hesitation, any shadow of doubt. *"You may dwell within the mansion, commune with those who find refuge within its enigmatic walls, but you shall never again tread upon the soils of your Earthly home, never again bask in the familiar embrace of a world once known. Can you, Itta, willingly imprison yourself within this enchanted realm, forsake all others to exist solely within the boundaries of our undying love?"*

Her gaze, once serene and steadfast, quivered ever so

slightly beneath the weight of his words, the realization of eternal isolation gently cracking the firmament of her resolve. A tear, a crystalline embodiment of love, sacrifice, and the melancholy beauty of eternal farewells, cascaded gently down her cheek.

As she pondered the precipice of eternity, Slyphor waited, a silent sentinel amidst the enchanted glade, ready to embrace her entirely or release her unto the fates, bound by the unspoken oath etched within the essence of his being: to love, honor, and protect, in this world and all others, across the boundless expanse of time.

Finally, she spoke, her voice a gentle cascade of vulnerability and steadfast conviction weaving through the charged silence of the glade.

"Slyphor, my beloved," Itta began, the gentle timbre of her voice embracing the stillness, "from the moment our souls whispered across the dimensions, from the first tendrils of our connection twined through the vast expanse separating our existences, I knew . . . I knew you were my destiny."

Her eyes, deep pools of dense emotion, held his, unflinching, as she continued. "This world, this Earthly realm from which I have sprung, it has never truly been my home. I have wandered its landscapes, basked in its beauties, and yet, always, there has been this . . . void, an insatiable yearning for something more, something beyond the tangible and transient."

She stepped forward, the delicate fabric of her ceremonial gown whispering against the verdant potpourri beneath her feet, hand reaching out to tenderly caress the ethereal aura surrounding him. "In you, I have found that elusive more, that eternal something which my soul has sought since the dawn of my existence."

A delicate, bittersweet smile caressed her lips, her words weaving an intricate tapestry of love, sacrifice, and eternal commitment. "I do not choose this path in spite of the chains that bind it, my love, but because of them. Because every link is forged from the love that courses through us, because every shackle is a testament to the depth, the intensity, the eternity of our bond."

Her fingers, gentle and trembling, sought his, intertwining with the spectral beauty of his being, the mingling of their energies igniting a cascade of celestial light, illuminating the glade with the undying flame of their love.

"I choose you, Slyphor. I choose us. I willingly embrace the bonds, the eternal confinement within this spectral realm, not as a prisoner, but as a fervent disciple of our love. This glade, this eternal moment suspended between realms, it shall be our sanctuary, our unending testament to a love unbounded by time or tether."

Tears, crystalline rivers of joy, sorrow, and unbridled love, traced rivulets down her cheeks, and yet, her gaze remained unwavering, her resolve unbroken amidst the burgeoning squall of their impending union. "I forsake the mortal coil, the Earthly realm, and willingly entwine my fate with yours, my beloved, for in you, I have found my home, my purpose, my eternity. I am yours, utterly and forevermore, bound by the heart, the soul, and the ethereal chains of our undying love."

And there, amidst the eternal twilight of the enchanted glade, Slyphor gazed upon his beloved, her words, her pledge, and her sacrifice igniting the embers of hope, commitment, and an all-consuming love within the shadowed recesses of his heart. Her decision, her willing submission to an eternity intertwined, offered both liberation and confinement, a paradox of emotion that would become the pulsating heartbeat of their immortal existence.

As Slyphor looked into Itta's eyes, he saw reflections of unending epochs, epochs that would be witnessed only by them, in a realm that obeyed no linear progression of moments. A gentle breeze, a whisper from the universe, rustled through the ancient, knowing trees of the glade, sealing their fates in a cocoon of eternity, as they prepared to step forward.

The glowing thread that had circled him for days intertwined around him once more, reaching out over the curves of Itta. It flickered and shone as they both watched it dance around them. The thread curled under her breasts and around her shoulders. It snaked up her neck and down her spine. It lit up the fabric of her gown and shined a light on her full body waiting for him.

The thread looped around her arms and guided her back on a soft mound the clearing must have put together for them. Slyphor stayed standing, tall, chest heaving, cock throbbing. *His Itta.* She was about to be his. Her nipples hardened and peaked underneath the sheer fabric, their dark color a contrast to her creamy skin.

Itta lay back on the altar for him. Her breasts heavy and full, her breathing slow and deep. She watched as Slyphor took tentative steps toward her, his large cock swaying with each step. She swallowed, eyes locked on his.

"Claim me," Itta whispered through the night air. "Mark me as yours. You are my creature, and I am ready for you."

FIFTEEN

The magic in the air grew tangible, a living force that coiled and surged around them. Even the ancient trees of the forest held their breath, their leaves quivering in anticipation. The Earth beneath their feet thrummed with an energy, a shuddering resonance as if the planet itself awaited this sacred union with bated breath.

All sounds of the night ceased, as if nature itself had stilled to bear witness. The chirping of crickets, the distant hoot of an owl, and even the gentle rustle of the wind through the leaves came to a halt, replaced by a charged silence, thick with expectancy.

During this profound stillness, Itta laid back, her heart's rhythm the only sound daring to pierce the quiet. But it wasn't one of fear. It was one of realization, recognition, and resolve. Every event in her life, every dream, every whisper of fate led her to this singular, monumental moment.

She felt the threads of time, destiny, and love intertwining around her, pulling her closer to her ethereal partner. The weight of generations of her family pulsed through her veins, their legacy urging her forward, their spirits surrounding her in silent support.

Deep down, a force stirred within her, an ancient power that had long been dormant. It was as if her soul recognized its purpose, its place in the vast tapestry of the universe. This wasn't just about love or duty. It was about destiny. Itta's entire existence, every breath she had taken, had prepared her for this pivotal juncture.

She was ready. Ready to embrace her fate, to protect the legacy woven through her lineage for millennia, and to unite with the creature who had become the other half of her soul.

Slyphor advanced, his presence now magnified, casting an imposing shadow over Itta as she reclined on the mound. She was a willing offering to their shared magic, a lamb ready to be devoured. His muscular legs seemed rooted in the Earth, while his chest rose and fell with fervor. Radiating a luminescent midnight hue, his figure was simultaneously solid at its core yet formless at the fringes.

His large arms flexed as he brought himself down closer to Itta and rested his palms on either side of her body. Slyphor inhaled deeply as he breathed in her smell. The flutter of his breath tickled her ears, her collarbone, her breasts.

"I am going to claim every last inch of you as mine. I will mark every pore of your skin. And when my cock is finally inside you, I will mark your soul." Slyphor's threat made Itta shudder with warmth and anticipation.

Itta grinned up at him and said, "Then do it."

Slyphor gripped the fabric of the veil tightly, shredding it with his hands and tossing it to the side. Itta's body lay arched on the mound, skin glowing, wetness pooling in between her legs. Slyphor surveyed her once more before tightly gripping her thighs and squeezing, pushing her knees out wide.

A moan escaped Itta's mouth as Slyphor stepped forward, pressing his hips against the back of her thighs. She could feel the heat of his cock as he ground himself against her middle. Itta felt the length of him slide in between her cheeks and she shuddered.

"You are not ready for me yet, my love." Slyphor chuckled at her eagerness.

"Then make me ready, Slyphor." Itta groaned. "Put your fingers inside me."

"I will do whatever you say for the rest of eternity," Slyphor whispered in her ear as he slowly slid in one thick finger and settled it deep inside her.

Itta's breath came out in gasps as the finger widened and pumped in and out of her. His finger seemed to shift and reshape itself as it pounded into her. Deep ridges rubbed against her walls as he ground his hand against her. The tip of it grew and widened as he slid his finger out, only to press it back in excruciatingly slow.

She was dripping wet, covering his hand. Her core was trembling.

"I must make it bigger, my love. So that you are ready,"

Slyphor whispered from above her, his attention focused on her core.

"Do it," she demanded.

Itta sat up on her elbows and watched as Slyphor's finger turned into the size of a very large human cock. She watched herself widen around him and take him in, inch by inch. Slyphor trailed his other fingers, these mercifully were still a normal size, to her backside.

He gripped her cheeks with force, lifting her up off the mound as he continued to ravage her, his hand pumping rapidly. Itta gasped as she felt a small pressure at her backside. Slyphor slipped a small finger in the tight muscle.

"Oh, god, I—"

The pressure inside Itta was mounting. The fullness she felt in her core was overwhelming. She threw herself onto his hand over and over again. She could feel the warmth in her belly expand. And when Slyphor shoved his hand in deeply and hooked his finger up to just the right spot she came undone.

Itta moaned and whimpered as waves of pleasure racked through her core. Her muscles gripped his finger, not wanting to let it go. Her vision blurred and she felt light-headed. Itta let out deep breaths as Slyphor slowly slid his fingers out of her. As soon as he was out of her, she craved his fullness again.

"Please, I need you inside me. Please, I'm ready, I promise," Itta begged for his cock.

"Tell me if it's too much and I will stop. Promise me."

Slyphor gripped his cock in his hand and stroked himself. He tapped himself at her entrance and she moaned.

"I will," Itta said. Then she took a deep breath as Slyphor pushed past her folds.

She was stretched and already so wet for him and it still felt like a shock. The pressure. The weight. The length. He spread her impossibly wide as he settled deep inside her.

"Breathe for me, love," Slyphor whispered from above.

Itta unclenched her jaw and let out a long breath. She felt the last couple of inches of him slide in. She wasn't sure she was going to be able to take all of him. He was impossibly thick and unnaturally long. Slyphor stood above her, still for a minute, allowing her to adjust.

Once Itta's breathing returned to normal, she rocked against him. She pushed herself back over the mound then back down onto him. He hit all the right places inside of her. She could feel him everywhere.

"I want you closer. I want to touch you. I want to feel more of you," Itta whispered through the night air.

In a swift movement, Slyphor gathered her up and spun them around. He sat on the edge of the mound with Itta's knees resting wide on his thighs. He pressed his mouth against her breasts, cupping them roughly with his hands.

Itta placed her hands on his chest as she lifted herself up only to lower herself back down on him. Her skin was glistening with sweat, but she wanted more. She finally found a rhythm and began bouncing on his cock.

"You take me so well, Itta. After tonight you will be ready for me always." He placed kisses on her jaw and licked a path

up her throat. *"The way I will fuck you will bring the trees down in this forest."*

Itta slammed herself down on him, feeling him reach places inside her she didn't think were possible. She gripped his neck and brought his face to hers. Itta found his eyes and locked onto them.

"Look around, my love. Look at what we have created."

Itta's gaze lingered, absorbing the altered ambience of the clearing. The metamorphosis in the magic was evident, as if the very fabric of the universe was adjusting to their union. The golden thread, once a mere whisper of ethereal connection, now danced vividly around the perimeter of the glade. It wove intricate patterns, embracing tree trunks and caressing the underbelly of leaves, and even burrowing through the rich Earth beneath the verdant carpet of grass, leaving a trail of soft luminescence in its wake.

The heavens themselves seemed to be participating in this cosmic event. The stars, those distant beacons of ancient light, felt intimately close tonight. They descended slightly, their twinkling intensities casting a dreamy illumination across the expanse, making the night feel both vast and intimate simultaneously.

Each element that Itta had meticulously arranged resonated with life. The crystals, herbs, and ancient symbols all shimmered with an inner fire, each pulsation synchronized to the rhythm of the universe. The ceremonial pieces, which once lay dormant and inanimate, now thrummed with raw energy, singing a silent symphony of ancient rites and promises.

"It's beautiful," Itta whispered.

"Are you ready for the next phase, my love?"

Itta looked at Slyphor in confusion. He gripped her backside and brought her down on him, leaning in to whisper in her ear.

"As much as I enjoy fucking you, the magic won't lock into place until I spill myself inside you. It's waiting for me, Itta. Are you ready?"

Itta placed her hand over his chest where she could feel the soft beating of his creature heart. She grabbed his hand and brought his palm over her own chest. She nodded.

With one hand on her heart and another gripping her waist, Slyphor pounded himself into her.

"Open your eyes. Watch what happens when I come inside you, Itta."

Itta threw her eyes open and as Slyphor roared she felt hot streams of his come fill her insides. As he exploded the woods shifted. Before Itta's eyes, the unimaginable occurred.

The Earth beneath them swayed, and the towering trees around them lifted their roots from the ground, leaves shaking in astonishment. The woods, in an act of ethereal wonder, turned on its axis, each tree, shrub, and blade of grass slowly rotating to find itself suspended in an inverted world. The ground now loomed overhead, a canopy of dirt, rocks, and roots, while the once-high treetops formed a new, surreal underbrush below.

This otherworldly sight was bathed in an iridescent glow. Every leaf, twig, and stone shimmered with a luminescence, casting spectral shadows that danced and twirled in the inverted landscape. It was a dreamscape of shifting realities, where up was down and the impossible was made real.

But the gravity-defying moment was short-lived. With a resonating sigh, the forest began its descent, turning itself right side up once more. Trees rooted themselves back into the Earth, the luminous glow fading as the woods settled back into its familiar, albeit forever changed, state.

Yet, for all its momentary chaos, the woods had undergone an indelible transformation. This ethereal event signaled the dawning of a new epoch, the flipping of an ancient hourglass that marked the commencement of their immortal stewardship. The forest had recognized, acknowledged, and celebrated their union, and in its own magnificent manner, sealed their fate as eternal guardians of this enchanted realm.

Itta sat on Slyphor's lap, him softening inside her slightly, hands around his neck. They found each other's eyes and smiled, communicating in a way only they understood. Itta was his now and he was hers. She placed a kiss on his mouth, hoping to feel him harden inside her again. She wanted more, craved more.

But then the atmosphere in the glade rapidly changed. A sizzling heat permeated the air, causing sweat to bead upon Itta's brow. The chill of the night was swallowed by a fierce, searing warmth.

The grass beneath them crisped and dried, and the dew that had settled on the leaves evaporated instantly. The golden threads of magic that had intertwined throughout the glade shimmered with an intensified heat, vibrating with unease.

In an instant, Slyphor lifted Itta and set her down on the mound beneath him, shielding her with his body. His form shifted into something larger and the soft look in his eyes was replaced with hardness.

From the midst of the now-steaming forest, a fiery figure emerged. Trails of smoke and embers trailed behind him as the ground where he stepped blistered and charred. It was the manifestation of the Fire element, an entity of blazing fury and unyielding heat.

SIXTEEN

With a voice that crackled like burning timber, the Fire element roared, *"Slyphor, you think your newfound bond can stand against me? You think a mere ceremony can deter my claim?"*

Itta tightened her grip on the mound, her eyes wide in a mix of fear and defiance. Slyphor's form hardened, his ethereal edges sharpening like forged steel, ready for a confrontation.

The Fire element continued, his flames licking higher and wilder with each word. *"This realm was promised to me in ages past, a debt that has been denied for far too long. The former guardians made a pact, and it's high time that debt was paid. I will take what is rightfully mine."*

The air grew thick with tension as the elemental forces of the glade—the Earth, the Water, the Wind, and now Fire—all stood in delicate balance. The pivotal moment had come.

Would the new bond between Itta and Slyphor hold strong against this fiery adversary?

With the mounting tension in the air, the manifestation of the Fire element grew fiercer, his flames roaring with increased intensity. While he didn't have a definitive form, the embodiment of Fire danced menacingly across the glade, scorching every bit of foliage it touched. Trees charred and flowers wilted as the Fire left a trail of destruction in its wake.

"Fyrian!" Slyphor boomed, using the ancient name of the Fire element. *"Your claims are based on deceit! The realm was never yours to claim."*

The dancing flames flared into a semi-humanoid form. Fyrian's voice, full of heat and anger, shot back, *"It was promised to me by Doran, the former guardian. He understood the power of Fire and recognized my rightful place."*

Slyphor's voice grew icy in contrast to Fyrian's heat. *"Doran was a renegade, he defied the ancient magics, disrespected the lineage. His word holds no weight here. He promised what was not his to give."*

The glade trembled as the energies clashed, with the wind blowing fiercely, trying to extinguish the flames, and the ground shaking with turmoil. The surrounding Waterin the glade steamed and hissed, ready to come to Slyphor's aid if needed.

"But you," Fyrian growled, *"you were lax. The rules were clear: Find your mate or forfeit the realm. You've overstepped, Slyphor, squandering the grace given to you."*

"I have found her now," Slyphor replied, his eyes fixed on

Itta with an intensity that sent shivers down her spine, a reaffirmation of their bond.

Fyrian's flames blazed brighter, and his voice filled with mockery. *"A little too late, don't you think? Maybe it's time for a new ruler, one who understands power and timing. I bet I could make your little plaything burn for me."*

In a move too fast for human eyes, Fyrian lashed out, a whip of Fire extending toward Itta, aiming to harm, to mark. Slyphor, in an instant, was there, his form acting as a barrier. The unEarthly shield absorbed the fiery whip, but Slyphor strained against the sheer force of it.

"You dare threaten her?" Slyphor roared, his voice echoing throughout the glade. His entire being surged with energy, and a massive ethereal blade manifested in his hand. The air crackled with magic as Slyphor and Fyrian collided, the fate of the realm hanging in the balance.

Amidst the tumultuous clash of elemental forces, Itta felt an overwhelming uncertainty gnawing at her core. Here she was, freshly bound in an ancient ritual, tossed into a fray she had little understanding of. Doubt clouded her thoughts. Was she truly ready for this? What if she failed?

Itta climbed to the top of the mound. The plush moss soft on her bare feet. A velvet cloak appeared over her shoulders, covering her naked body.

As the clamor intensified, a sudden tranquility washed over her. She felt a presence, ethereal and maternal, soothing her turbulent emotions. The voice of her ancestor, a powerful matriarch from epochs past, whispered in her ear,

"Itta, my child, you are the culmination of generations, the embodiment of our legacy. They are the guardians, yes, but you are the magic."

Memories, not her own, flooded her consciousness. Visions of past ceremonies, of guardians and trials, of victories and lessons passed down. She saw her foremothers, each a beacon of strength and wisdom, standing tall amidst their own challenges.

With newfound clarity, Itta felt an overwhelming surge of energy coursing through her veins. The ancestral knowledge and power of her lineage beckoned her to act. With each breath, she drew from the depths of her being, echoing the chants and spells she had unknowingly carried within her all her life.

She chanted, her voice growing in strength, the ancient words resonating with the magic of the glade. Each phrase was a testament to her lineage, to the women who came before her and the legacy they entrusted to her. The energy she unleashed, pure and potent, shaped the fate of the glade.

With each word, the imbalance caused by Fyrian's rage began to rectify. The glade responded to her call, recognizing its true master. The very essence of this realm resonated with her voice, harmonizing with her desires.

Slyphor and Fyrian, lost in their elemental battle, sensed the shift. Their conflict paled in comparison to the power Itta now wielded. As the magic enveloped the clearing, Fyrian's flames dimmed, while Slyphor's form shimmered with awe and reverence.

Itta stood tall, her silhouette a beacon against the chaotic backdrop. The pulsating energy around her amplified, causing ripples in the fabric of the realm. Her eyes, once clouded with doubt, now gleamed with unyielding confidence and determination. Her posture radiated power—the power of a lineage that was ancient, pure, and undiluted. This wasn't just about her and Slyphor or even the raging Fyrian. This was about preserving a legacy.

"The magic of this realm," she began, her voice carrying an authority both startling and inspiring, "is not merely a tool to be wielded by those who seek power. It is a birthright, a responsibility. It is an honor that demands respect, not just from the guardians but from all who walk these lands."

As she spoke, the glade shimmered with ethereal light. From the depths of the forest, figures emerged. Each pair, male and female, represented an element—their attire and aura reflecting the essence they guarded. The women's dresses flowed like water, their hair shimmered like fire, and their eyes held the depth of the Earth and the lightness of air. Though partnered, it was the women who bore the core of the elemental magic.

Each elemental pairing had its dynamics. While the men held a reservoir of latent energy, it was the women who acted as the conduit, channeling and focusing that power. Without them, the magic was directionless and risked withering away.

The matriarchs of Water, Earth, and Air stepped forth, their male counterparts respectfully behind them, acknowledging their pivotal role. Seraphine of Water, Tera of Earth, and Aeoliana of Air—each held a gaze deep with wisdom and strength.

Seraphine's voice was melodic as she addressed the gathering: "We are not damsels to be shielded. We are the heartbeats of these elements. The men, our counterparts, amplify our might, but we are the bearers of this legacy."

Tera, her voice grounding and resonating with the depth of the Earth, added, "We need not protection, but partnership. A collaborative dance that keeps the balance of this realm intact."

Aeoliana's voice was a gentle breeze, yet firm in its message: "Our power, when combined, is unparalleled. But divided, it fades. This realm thrives on unity."

Itta took a step forward, her aura brightening. "The essence of collaboration is understanding and respect. Men of the elements, remember your roles. Stand beside us, not in front. Support us, do not overshadow. The magic of this realm is a delicate tapestry weaved by both. But the threads are held by the matriarchs. Choose to work in harmony, or face banishment from this sacred space."

The message was clear: The balance of the realm depended on the combined strength and collaboration of both male and female guardians. The magic was a shared responsibility, but the true keepers, the heart of it all, were the women.

The assembly was held in rapt attention as Itta's words echoed, ringing with unerring truth. The air hummed in agreement, each element paying heed to the fundamental truths she laid bare.

Beside the elemental pairs, the denizens of the forest watched—creatures of myths, sprites, and fae. They too were tethered to this realm's balance, and its fate was intertwined with their existence. The luminous eyes of will-o'-the-wisps, the gentle rustling of dryad wings, and the whispered murmurs of nymphs and sprites all added to the living tapestry of the glade.

Near the water's edge, ancient tortoises bearing runes on their shells nodded in agreement, their long lives making them witnesses to countless ceremonies, pacts, and battles for power. Their aged eyes reflected the wisdom of eons, understanding the importance of the balance Itta championed.

Perched on gnarled branches, wise old owls hooted softly, the bright moonlight illuminating their feathers, turning them into shimmering guardians of the night. Their keen eyes observed, acknowledging the truth in Itta's words.

Beneath the surface of the glade's waters, silvery merfolk watched, their scales reflecting the ethereal lights of the glade. They whispered among themselves, their voices harmonizing with the gentle lull of the water.

As Fyrian's flames dimmed further, his voice, though subdued, still carried a tone of defiance. *"The past cannot be erased. Promises were made, and they demand reparation."*

Itta responded, her voice gentle yet firm, "The past is a lesson, not a chain. Doran's promises were empty, born from deceit and greed. But we can choose a different path, one of unity and collaboration."

Fyrian, his form flickering, seemed torn. The weight of history bore down on him, but so did the undeniable truth of the present. He looked at Itta, the embodiment of centuries of elemental magic, and saw a glimmer of hope. Perhaps there was a way to heal the wounds of the past without the realm tearing itself apart.

Slyphor, still vigilant, stepped beside Itta, offering Fyrian a nod of respect. *"The path of confrontation leads to ruin for all. Let's seek understanding, a way to coexist."*

Among the assembly, murmurs of agreement grew. Many remembered the times when elements clashed, resulting in devastation. They did not wish for a repeat of those dark times.

The glade seemed to sense the shift in sentiments. The air grew lighter, the waters clearer, and even the ground pulsated with life. The vibrant flora regained its colors, pushing back against the scars left by Fyrian's flames.

Itta, her voice a soothing balm, concluded, "This realm thrives when we act as stewards, not conquerors. Let us renew our vows, to protect, to nurture, and to respect the delicate balance that sustains us all."

With that, the elemental guardians, both old and new, came together. They began a ritual, one of unity and promise, weaving their magic into a protective shield around the glade.

The spectacle was breathtaking. Streams of light intertwined, forming intricate patterns in the sky. Every creature, every being, every element in the glade contributed to this shared symphony of magic and intent.

As dawn approached, the glade was transformed beyond

a place of magic, a testament to the possibility of harmony, even amidst the trials of history and the uncertainties of the future. The guardians, with Itta and Slyphor at the helm, had reaffirmed their commitment, ensuring the realm's magic would endure for generations to come.

Dearest Aether,

As the Winter Solstice approaches and the realm is cloaked in a blanket of frost and stillness, I find myself enveloped in a warmth that emanates from within. It's been but a few days since that pivotal moment, yet the feelings it ignited within me have grown, expanded, and matured.

In the presence of Itta, every nuance of the universe seems magnified, every whisper of the Windmore profound. There's a depth to my emotions I hadn't anticipated. Beyond the passion and the union, there's an undercurrent of awe, a deep-seated reverence for the woman she is and the bond we now share.

This isn't merely about the power she wielded that night or the legacy she upheld; it's about the vulnerability, the trust, and the unyielding strength she exhibited. Her actions served as a mirror, reflecting to me the true essence of love—not just as an emotion but as a force, a transformative power that melds, nurtures, and transcends.

Dearest Aether, with the solstice upon us, marking the end of one cycle and the beginning of another, I feel reborn. Reborn into a love that promises not just companionship but also growth, understanding, and a journey of discovery.

Tomorrow, as the realm acknowledges the shortest day and the longest night, I will stand beside Itta, hand in hand, ready to welcome the new dawn and all the mysteries it holds. The solstice signifies renewal, and I find it fitting that it comes so close on the heels of the profound shift in my life.

Thank you, Aether, for being my eternal confidante. Tonight, as I bask in the glow of love, I send out a silent prayer of gratitude to the cosmos, feeling immensely blessed to have Itta by my side.

With warmth and reverence,
Slyphor

EIGHTEEN

The mansion was abuzz with preparations. The grand hallways echoed with laughter and music, the scent of pine and winterberries filled the air, and intricate snowflake patterns adorned the elaborate chandeliers. Everywhere she looked, the decorations whispered of ancient traditions and joyous celebrations. This was the day of the Winter Solstice, a time of renewal and togetherness, and the entire realm seemed to be holding its breath in anticipation.

Itta walked through the mansion with a heart full of emotions.

Today was not only about the solstice but also about a deeply personal reunion. Her family would be arriving soon.

She remembered the last time she'd seen her mother and Ondina. It had been a whirlwind of emotions as she'd bid them farewell, stepping into the unknown journey that had led her here. It had already felt like a lifetime ago since she had hugged them, and she wondered if they would be able to notice the shifts that have taken place.

Her thoughts drifted to the women of the clearing. After the ritual, she had spent time getting to know each of them, delving into their lives and the responsibilities they held. Their stories were intriguing, and the bond they shared was undeniable. They were guardians, women of great power, and Itta felt humbled to be part of such a lineage.

One name she had often heard whispered with great respect was Aelia, the former guardian of the Wind element. While Itta hadn't had the privilege of meeting her, tales of Aelia's dedication, grace, and serene presence reverberated through the stories the guardians shared. It was said that Aelia had served her post for a millennium with great diligence, later transitioning to her peaceful immortal life, leaving the Wind post vacant and in search of its new guardian.

Itta had connected deeply with the other elements and their guardians, finding solace in their shared responsibilities and mutual respect. The tales of Seraphine, the Water guardian, particularly intrigued her. Seraphine had three male guardians who watched over her—a unique arrangement in the world of elemental guardians. Their bond was a testament to the strength and depth of the Water element, emphasizing its significance in the balance of the realm.

With each passing day, Itta grew stronger, absorbing the knowledge and experiences of the guardians. The sense of purpose and responsibility weighed on her, but she was not alone. The companionship and mentorship of the guardians were her pillars of strength, guiding her through her new life.

As she snapped back to the present, she wondered how she would share all of this with Ondina. Would her sister understand? Would she see the changes that had taken place in her? Only time would tell. For now, Itta was eager to embrace her family and celebrate the Winter Solstice, surrounded by love and warmth.

By nightfall, once her family had tired itself on food and wine, she'd venture into the clearing in search of Slyphor. Itta craved him insatiably. Her insides hummed for him. Her body craved him. She'd find herself lost in thought, wetness beginning to pool between her legs, when she'd be brought back to the present with the clinking of a glass or bout of laughter down the hall.

"Ready for more already, my love?" Slyphor's voice came filtering in through her thoughts. Even though he wasn't in front of her, he was always around. Teasing her, feeling her through their shared bond.

Itta was ready to run off to the clearing to find a quick release when she heard chatter at the front door. Her mother and sister were here.

The excitement building up inside Itta overflowed when she heard the familiar tones of her family at the entrance. She hurried down the winding staircase, her feet barely touching the ground, and as she turned the corner, she was met with the familiar and comforting sight of her mother and Ondina.

Ondina, with her radiant smile and sparkling eyes, was the first to spot her. "Itta!" she exclaimed, rushing forward to envelop her sister in a tight embrace. Their mother, a graceful woman with strands of silver in her hair that hinted at her age, joined in the hug, and for a moment, the world outside shrunk to the three of them, bound by blood and love.

Itta gently took Ondina by the hand, her fingers tingling with the urge to share all that had occurred. "Come," she whispered, leading her younger sister through the large double doors and out onto the grounds. As they walked side by side, the golden hues of the setting sun bathed the gardens in a warm, ethereal glow. The two women wound their way through ancient trees, past shimmering ponds and blossoming flowers that nodded in acknowledgment of the solstice.

Meanwhile, their mother gracefully made her way through the mansion, seeking out her own sister to see where she might be of assistance. The house was indeed alive with anticipation. Staff bustled about, making final adjustments to the décor; musicians tuned their instruments; and from the kitchens came the delectable aroma of festive dishes being prepared.

Outside, Itta recounted her experiences, her words flowing like a melodious river. Ondina listened with rapt attention, her eyes widening with wonder and occasionally misting over with emotion. Every so often, the younger sister would interject with questions, her curiosity about the magical world her elder sister had become a part of evident.

It felt liberating for Itta to share everything—the guardians, the rituals, and her deepening connection to the elements. They paused beneath an ancient oak, its boughs heavy with snow, and Itta took a deep breath, reveling in the shared moment.

Ondina squeezed Itta's hand, her voice soft. "I'm so proud of you," she murmured. "And a little envious. Your journey . . . it's like something out of our childhood fairy tales."

Itta chuckled softly, her heart full. "It feels that way sometimes," she admitted. "But it's also very real. And I can't wait for you to see some of it tonight."

The two continued their walk, the bond between them stronger than ever, as they looked forward to the night's celebrations and the magic it promised to bring.

As the last hues of sunlight bled into the horizon, the realm took on a dreamlike quality. The expansive grounds, blanketed in a layer of freshly fallen snow, shimmered under the emerging twilight. The silvered trees stood as silent sentinels, their branches adorned with tiny, luminous crystals that caught the dimming light, creating a soft, otherworldly glow.

The mansion's residents and guests, draped in festive garments of deep blues, silvers, and golds, made their way outside. A path had been cleared, leading to a vast, circular clearing where the solstice ceremony would take place. In the center of this clearing stood a grand, ancient stone altar, engraved with symbols that told tales of ages past.

It was a tradition in the realm to mark the Winter Solstice with the "Ceremony of Light and Renewal." This rite celebrated the return of longer days, the victory of light over darkness, and the promise of rejuvenation for the land and its inhabitants.

As everyone gathered around the altar, a hush fell upon the crowd. Itta's mother and aunt, being the elders of the family, stepped forward. With practiced grace, they began the ritual.

First, they lit a large, braided candle placed at the center of the altar, representing unity and the intertwining of light and dark. As the flame took hold, its bright light symbolized the returning sun, its warmth promising a new beginning.

Next, each participant was handed a small crystal vial containing a luminescent liquid—the Essence of Aether. One by one, they approached the altar and poured their vial onto the flame, causing it to change colors and emit mesmerizing patterns of light. This act signified the merging of individual energies with the collective, reinforcing the bond of the community.

Itta and Ondina approached together. As Itta poured her essence, the flame danced with silvery wisps and swirling grays, reflecting her connection to the wind. Ondina's contribution made the flame shimmer with deep blues and aqua tones, a testament to her own latent magical affinities.

Finally, as the last of the essence was added, and the altar's flame reached its zenith, a choral group sang an ancient hymn. Their voices rose in perfect harmony, weaving a tapestry of sound that seemed to lift the spirits of all who heard it.

The Ceremony of Light and Renewal was not just an ode to the solstice, but a reminder of the cyclical nature of life. As the flame dimmed, returning to its original warm glow, the participants knew that even in the darkest times, light would always find its way back.

The vast expanse of the sky above slowly transitioned from a deep twilight blue to the inky black of night, punctuated by a million glittering stars. Gentle notes from the choral group filled the cold night air, their voices blending seamlessly with the soft rustling of leaves and the distant murmurs of the guests.

Itta felt a mysterious pull, a soft tug at the core of her being. Even amid the throng of family and familiar faces, the sensation of Slyphor's presence surrounded her, like an unseen embrace, a whisper of a breeze that only she could discern. Although he remained concealed, she could sense his watchful gaze from the shadows, his energy wrapping around her like a protective cocoon.

As the final notes of the song faded, Ondina leaned closer, her voice hushed with wonder. "This world, Itta . . . it's beyond anything I could have imagined. And to think you're at the heart of it."

Itta smiled softly, her gaze distant. "It's a responsibility, but one I'm proud to bear."

The sisters shared a lingering embrace, the warmth of the connection palpable. As they moved toward the mansion, Ondina paused, her gaze searching the trees and shadows. "He's here, isn't he?" she whispered with a knowing smile. Itta, her face illuminated with a soft blush, merely nodded.

Understanding the deep connection her sister had forged with the Guardian of the Wind, Ondina's eyes sparkled with mischief. "Go," she encouraged gently, "I can see that pull in your eyes. Just promise to share more tales tomorrow."

Itta grinned, squeezing her sister's hand in gratitude. "I promise."

As the crowd dispersed, making their way back to the warmth of the grand house, Itta lingered a moment longer, her gaze drawn to the edge of the woods. She could feel him, his vast presence beyond the tree line, waiting patiently for their moment of reunion.

With the mansion's lights twinkling in the distance and the soft glow of the solstice flame behind her, she made her way toward the tree line. The anticipation built with each step, her heart racing with excitement.

The world blurred around her until, emerging from the shadows, Slyphor's grand form materialized. The intensity of his gaze met hers, and in that instant, all the events of the day melted away, leaving only the two of them, bound by a love that transcended time and realms.

Tonight marked not only the rebirth of the sun but also the next chapter in their intertwined destinies. The Winter Solstice was just the beginning.

NINETEEN

The woods around the mansion were dense and enigmatic, each tree and shadow holding tales of old. But as Itta followed Slyphor deeper into the forest, the familiar terrain gave way to the mystical glade of the clearing. This was a place of power, a nexus of elemental energy where the air pulsed with magic. Tonight, it was alive in a way Itta had never seen before.

The glade was bathed in an iridescent glow, emanating from hundreds of softly glowing orbs floating effortlessly above. These orbs, reminiscent of fireflies, cast a soft light that danced and played upon the couples spread throughout the clearing. Each pair was deeply engrossed in their own ceremony, seeking both to give and receive from the ancient magic of the land.

The sight was mesmerizing: couples of all backgrounds and walks of life, each exuding a profound intimacy as they sought to replenish their magic. Some stood face-to-face, their hands clasped as they exchanged whispered words and soft touches. Others danced in slow, synchronized movements, their forms casting long, intricate shadows. Still, others tentatively explored each other, hands roaming over bodies.

On the edge of the clearing stood a majestic stone obelisk, taller than the surrounding trees, its surface etched with runes that shimmered and shifted. This monument was the head of the glade, channeling the energies shared by the couples, directing it to the Earth and sky, ensuring the balance of magic in the realm.

Slyphor turned to Itta, his eyes intense and filled with emotion. *"Tonight, we are both giver and receiver,"* he whispered, the weight of his words settling around them. *"We are the magic that requires replenishment. Our bond, our connection, is what this realm feeds upon and, in turn, what grants it strength."*

Itta felt a swell of emotion as the truth of Slyphor's words settled in. Their bond was unique, a blend of raw elemental power and mystical love. Tonight, they would not just witness the ceremony but actively participate, fortifying not only their magic but that of the entire realm.

Itta's eyes swept across the gathering. Every face awaited her cue, filled with expectation. She stood at the forefront, the orchestrator. The commencement of the ceremony rested on her decision. Her heart pounded in her chest as excitement built in her belly.

Her hands reached for the tassel at her cloak, and she

pulled the gold threads apart, revealing a sheer white gown underneath. Her body shown through the fabric, a glimmering glow from the firelight. With a single tilt of her chin, she gave her signal.

The couples around her took their cue. Tentative touches turned intentional. Groups gathered in small clusters as bodies joined. Itta walked the circle of the glade like an overseer of sensuality. Her nods encouraged movements and her smile put her crowd at ease.

"You're a natural at this, my love," Slyphor's voice spoke through her mind.

"I don't know what I'm supposed to be doing," Itta admitted.

"You are free to participate in whatever way you like. Guide them. Join them. Show them. It is your ceremony, Itta."

Warmth flooded her belly at the thought. But she was nervous.

"Trust me, my love. Your magic will thank you. Try it, you will see. Start with them."

Itta was standing in front of a man and a woman. They sat side by side as his hands trailed up her arms and tugged gently at her hair. His mouth was on her neck as Itta knelt in front of them.

The couple's attention turned to Itta, grateful for her presence. The man's eyes took in Itta as the woman leaned forward, brushing a hand over Itta's cheek. Warmth immediately flooded Itta's core. It was as if she could feel the supply of her magic humming deep within her, craving more.

The woman got up on her knees and ran her hands over

Itta's breasts, letting them overflow in her hands. The magic flared and hummed. The woman placed her mouth gently on Itta's. The magic flickered.

Itta slid her tongue past her own teeth and into the warmth of the woman's mouth. She tasted of orange and cinnamon. A zap of magic coursed through Itta.

"That's it, my love. The more you receive, the more the magic will thank you." Slyphor's voice was a caress in her mind.

Itta brought her body closer to the woman's, feeling their breasts pressed up against each other. She roamed her hands over the woman's shoulders and down her waist. The man next to them had taken his cock out and was lazily stroking it as he watched them.

There was a buzzing in Itta, and it was addicting. She craved the feeling the magic was giving her and she wanted more of it. She guided the woman's hand down between her legs. The woman greedily took over at Itta's permission and soon Itta gasped as she felt the woman's fingers slide in between her folds.

"You are so beautiful, Itta. Do her fingers feel good inside you, my love?"

Itta answered with a moan that made the man pick up the speed at which he was tugging his cock. The woman continued sliding her fingers in and out. They were delicate and light in comparison to Slyphor's. Their touch featherlight against her skin. Itta clenched tightly around them when the woman used her other hand to sharply pinch her nipple.

Itta's breaths came out in huffs as the woman brought her closer and closer to the edge. The buzz of the magic kept intensifying.

"You don't have to hold on, Itta. You will come many times tonight. Come for her, my love."

Itta was glad she didn't have to hold on any longer. As the woman rubbed firm circles on her clit, Itta exploded. She heard the man beside them grunt his own release on to his belly, but Itta barely noticed.

As if the stars themselves had exploded inside Itta, her vision was blurred but colorful. Her skin tingly and warm. Her release brought her a high she had never experienced, and she was already craving more of it.

"Yes, Itta, the magic tonight is addicting. It is greedy and selfish and will keep demanding more until it is full. Let's give it what it wants."

Itta stood from the couple and made her way around the circle. There were couples in the throes of intimacy all around her and even the sight was enough to make the magic tingle.

"Go to him; he wants to taste you."

She let Slyphor guide her to a man sitting on a small boulder on the edge of the circle. His legs were out wide, his cock already hard and veiny in his hand. Itta stood in front of him, and he grinned up at her before burying his face in between her legs.

She let out a yelp as his tongue snaked its way up her middle, finding her soaking wet with her release. He hooked his fingers inside her to gather up her wetness and used it to coat his own cock as he continued to tug on it.

His large hand held her in place as his face, rough stubble coating his cheeks, continued to devour her. Itta gripped his hair and pulled him close, feeling his nose press against her swollen clit. God, she was already so close again.

"I want you, Slyphor. I am ready for you," Itta spoke to Slyphor in her mind.

"Almost, my love. You need to build your reserves first. Once I claim you tonight, they won't be able to touch you."

And so, Itta let the man, with the expert tongue, bring her to another orgasm. She shook and shuddered as he held her in place while he lapped up every ounce of her release. The magic buzzed stronger now from the deep recesses of her body, bringing her a euphoria she'd never known.

When Itta would've normally been exhausted and spent, she found energy. Every time she found a release, she felt replenished and fresh. Her body was overcome with pleasure by various members of the circle, all with Slyphor in her ear guiding her.

Finally, she felt the tap of her reserves fill completely. The lid on her magic seemingly shutting closed. It was time. She left the small group she was playing with, stood, and found Slyphor, in his form, waiting for her.

Leading her to the center of the clearing, surrounded by a ring of firelight, Slyphor gently took her hands. *"Our energies combined are potent,"* he said, his voice a soft murmur. *"We must give willingly, but in return, the magic will fortify us, making our bond even stronger."*

The energy of the circle shifted. What was once a frenzy of bodies and sounds and movements was now still. Waiting. For them.

Itta watched Slyphor's shape as he circled her. She could see his form reflected in the wide eyes of their specters. *Her creature.*

"Are you ready for me to take you in front of all these people? To claim you? To shove my cock inside you while everyone watches?" Slyphor's voice boomed through the clearing.

Itta nodded eagerly.

"Say it, Itta."

"Yes. I'm ready. I want you to take me. Fuck me. Right now." Itta's voice was breathless. Her body a ball of tingling nerves.

"Lie back."

Itta lay back on the mound in the center of the circle. Her naked body on full display. Each of her specters' eyes were on her. She was neither shy nor unabashed. Itta felt the power dripping off her like sweat so she took in her new role with pride. Slyphor walked over to her, gripping his massive cock in his hand. She could see the tip of it already glistening.

Itta slid her feet up the mound on either side of her and widened her legs. Her fingers danced down to her core, teasing him. She trailed a finger down her middle, widened her lips for him, and smiled.

And in one quick movement, he was sheathed inside her. His thick cock shoved past her entrance and settled into her wetness within. Slyphor scooped her up off the mound and held her in the air as he pounded into her. Her swollen breasts bounced, her long hair hung loose behind her.

As he fucked her, the guests all watched. Lazily stroking each other or sharing light kisses. They were spent but ready to watch the star of the show. For the final level of magic to be filled. For this night, with everything that was shared, would replenish their magic until the next Winter Solstice.

With Slyphor deep inside her, the world seemed to fade. Itta reveled in the profound connection to him, to the Earth beneath her feet, the sky above, and the fabric of the universe. Their energies intertwined, spiraling upward in a dance of light and shadow. It was a raw, powerful sensation, one of vulnerability and strength combined.

As dawn broke, with Slyphor pounding into her, the ceremony reached its crescendo. The stone obelisk at the head of the clearing pulsed with a brilliant light, drawing in all the shared energies and radiating it outward in waves. The ground vibrated, and the air shimmered with power.

And, finally, when Slyphor tensed and spilled himself inside her the stone broke out into a powerful glow. They were at the heart of the realm's magic, their love and bond the cornerstone upon which it thrived.

The glade emptied, couples leaving hand in hand, their magic replenished, and their connections deepened. But Itta and Slyphor lingered a little longer, basking in the afterglow of the ceremony and the profound change it had wrought upon them.

Tonight was a testament to the power of love, connection, and the ancient magic that bound them all. The realm would flourish, its magic vibrant and strong, all thanks to the sacrifices and connections made in this sacred glade.

To the Esteemed Aether,

The Winter Solstice has come and gone, and with it, the ceremony that had been the focal point of so many discussions and preparations. I find it necessary, nay, essential, to update you on the results of this monumental event.

Itta was the heart of the evening, and words might never capture the immensity of pride I felt seeing her at the helm. She stepped into her role, not hesitatingly, but as if she was made for this moment. To think of her journey, of the transformation she has undergone in such a short span, is to acknowledge a force of nature. She wields her power as one would a second skin, with a grace and confidence that left everyone, including myself, in awe.

There is an ancient deity, as you well know —the God of Serendipitous Ties, who is believed to bind souls in an eternal dance of love and destiny. My gratitude toward this deity knows no bounds, for if it is their design that Itta and I are connected, then I am forever in their debt. I often find myself pausing, reflecting on the beauty of fate, and how I have been blessed to find someone who fits so seamlessly into the tapestry of my existence.

As I watched her during the ceremony, I was astounded by her resilience and her intuitive understanding of what the magic demanded of her. There were moments where the sheer intensity of her presence made the air thrum with energy, every action resonating with purpose and conviction.

I cannot fathom the depth of my feelings toward Itta, and words often fall short. But I know this: the universe, in all its infinite wisdom, has granted me a gift that I cherish with every beat of my heart. I am humbled by the thought of spending eternity alongside her, exploring the myriad facets of our shared existence.

In conclusion, Aether, the ceremony was not just a success but a testament to Itta's inherent prowess and the depths of our bond. As we journey forward, with every rising sun and every waning moon, I remain ever hopeful and ever grateful for the love and magic that permeates our lives.

With Itta's ascendance and our unyielding bond, you can rest assured: the Wind Realm is now, and will remain, safely guarded.

With utmost respect and gratitude,
Slyphor

ACKNOWLEDGMENTS

Ah, here we are again. Whether you're here for your first read of my books, or you've fallen down the rabbit hole, thank you for being here and being *you*.

Since this is my last book to be published in 2023 (never fear there are plenty slated for next year and beyond!), I feel like I owe this one a love letter. This year, in general, wrecked me in so many ways. I will never understand how one year can hold the title as one of the worst and one of the best all in the same breath.

I'm so fucking honored to be on this journey and that YOU are here with me. I'll never take that for granted.

This book couldn't have been made possible without my absolute dream team. Caroline, Kimberly, and Molly - thank you for being the best editing team a girl could ever ask for. To my ARC Club - thank you for saying yes to all my wild and promiscuous ideas, I truly feel like we're just getting started. Thank you to my PR team and all the book accounts who have shared my work - you make me feel like I actually have a chance in this space.

To my family who lets me sneak away for coffee shop writing dates, ignores me when I space out thinking of a new scene, and who *thankfully* doesn't ask what I write about - I love you.

ABOUT THE AUTHOR

Gabi Salas, the mastermind behind sizzling contemporary romances, believes reading smut is feminist AF. She's the author of the debut series "The Prism Society," a solid one-handed read *wink*. Gabi resides in Kansas City with her husband, hilarious daughter, and a ridiculously cuddly cat named Pepper. When not crafting stories, she's  drowning in honey oat milk lattes, binging smutty novels, or dark and twisty murder podcasts. Connect at gabisalas.com